Nothin' But Sugar Copy

A Holiday Cozy
Cass Kim

Cass Kim LLC

Contents

Chapter One

"We need you out and ready in seven, Michaela," Bellamy called into the small trailer being used as a wardrobe, tapping on the flimsy aluminum door.

Two feet away another dressing room burst open and the long, tanned legs of Ally Bennicio wobbled down the metal steps, the four-inch stiletto heels strapped to her feet barely missing the asinine gaps in the grates. Nobody ever thought about the heels the models wore when they rented these cheap wardrobe boxes. Although lately, they were just lucky the trailers' AC could keep up with the baking LA sun. Summer had been a sweltering mess. Fall was... Well, Fall was a mess so far, too.

"Bellamy, oh thank goodness. I got this text from Amma and now I don't know what to do about tomorrow. You said I had it off! You said I could take the audition." Ally shoved her pink rhinestone-covered phone in Bellamy's face and hovered as Bellamy skimmed the text.

Tomorrow I need you at the perfume ad. You miss it, you're done. No back pay.

Bellamy swallowed hard. This wasn't the first time her boss Amma, the owner of Ammazing Models, had made illegal threats to the girls. A trickle of sweat skimmed down her spine. Amma would be retiring soon. She'd promised Bellamy would be taking over operations by no later than Thanksgiving. That moment would make all of the fourteen-plus hour days worth it. She'd have the chance to make the company a little better. A little kinder to the girls. A little safer. Definitely she would run it with fewer barking text message threats. But, for the next month and a half, she reminded herself, the time for making things better was not now. Right now, time was money.

"I—I can't fix this right now." Bellamy swallowed her frustration. She couldn't fix anything about the company until she was in the driver's seat of the business. "I'll try to talk to Amma later today." Bellamy shoved the sticky tendrils of hair escaping her bun off the back of her neck as she adjusted her tone from regret to business and reminded the model, "But for now...We need you on set, Ally." She glanced at the delicate gold watch on her right wrist. "Like, now. Robe off. Bikini only." She couldn't look at Ally as she said it.

They both knew the audition tomorrow wouldn't be happening for her, not if she wanted to be paid for her work today. Bellamy couldn't face the tears she was certain were shimmering in the eighteen-year-old's eyes. She knew they were there because a decade ago when she'd come to LA with nothing but long legs and big dreams, she'd faced the same hard choices. Eat tomorrow or bet it all on the smallest maybe.

Growling under her breath, she refused to waste any more paid photographer time wallowing over things she couldn't change. "Michela! Now!" Bellamy pounded on the thin metal door, then moved her hand to the latch. With so many people on set, she really tried not to open the doors to the dressing rooms She wasn't here to assist in any peep shows if the girls weren't fully changed. Michaela had been a model for the agency for over six years now. They both knew her time working for Ammazing Models was almost up. It wasn't lost on Bellamy that the twenty-five-year-old had been taking more time getting ready. Was late more often. Was barely more than skin and bones.

"Michaela, I'm coming in," Bellamy warned as she tugged at the plastic latch. It popped open with no response from the model within. Grunting, Bellamy hauled herself up the corrugated steps and into the cool darkness of the trailer. "Michaela? M, babe, I know you're mad that Ally's getting more jobs than you, but we really need you to get on set and—" As her eyes adjusted to the lack of sunlight, Bellamy could just make out the outline of one delicate wrist, the thin fingers curled slightly where they rested on the floor, unmoving in the partially opened doorway of the bathroom. Gasping, she dove to her knees, ignoring her designer pantsuit, and clasped the younger girl's hand.

"M?" She shook the hand slightly, then held her breath as she inched her fingers forward to the pulse point on her wrist. Bellamy knew she should be calling 911, but that part of her felt like it was nothing more than wispy clouds losing the battle against the burning sun of her panic. Relief burst through her as she felt the weak pop-pop-pop of blood thrusting its way through the model's veins. Inching the door open, Bellamy craned her head around to see if Michaela was clothed even as her other hand unlocked her cell phone to call for help.

Amma be damned. This photoshoot was over. Bellamy knew as she hit send that Amma would be lecturing her later on the expense of getting an ambulance on set. The loss of profit due to paying the models for the day even when things wrapped early. The waste of the photographers. Not to mention how angry the clients would be about this delay. Amma be damned.

Bellamy hit send.

"You realize that you've cost us this client, correct?" For a woman under five feet tall, Amma Peren was awfully intimidating.

Bellamy ducked her head, wishing she'd had time to change out of her sweaty pantsuit before being ambushed by Amma at the hospital.

"It seems you've lost your tongue in all of this."

Bellamy didn't have to look up to see her mentor's pursed lips and annoyed tapping of an unlit Marlboro menthol.

"You had plenty to say earlier when you told the crew to shut down. You didn't struggle at all to speak to the 911 operator, I'm certain," Amma continued. "You surely didn't hesitate to flush my business's name down the toilet along with that girl's coke habit." The velvet steel of Amma's voice forced Bellamy's eyes up.

"There wasn't any coke." The words felt explosive in the tiled hallway, the floors practically built to ricochet sound. "I told you before. Michaela doesn't do drugs. She doesn't deserve this. She did nothing wrong. I did nothing wrong."

"Is that so? You allowed one of my talents to get so skinny that she had a heart attack...without any drugs?" A bitter laugh, "Babe, if I'd had half your height and looks I'd have done a hell of a lot more with them. Wanna be actress, turned model, turned model herder." Amma arched one meticulously shaped brow. "And not even a good one at that."

"Soon to be agency manager, not model manager." Despite her eyebrows forcing themselves down, Bellamy kept her tone light, giving just enough emphasis on manager to let Amma know she wasn't going to let her forget her promises. "You booked her six days straight. You told her, more than once, that she's showing her age. Her age, Amma?" Bellamy swallowed, lowering her voice before adding, "She's barely twenty-five years old."

A nurse scooted past them, not bothering to hide her distaste for Amma, and by extension Bellamy. Straightening her shoulders Bellamy managed to dip her head in a passable nod of greeting. It was the same nurse who'd checked Michaela in. Who'd informed Bellamy that because of Michaela's low BMI and irregular pulse she'd be running heart checks in addition to providing IV hydration. The same nurse that made sure Bellamy knew how many models

they got each month with similar conditions sec-
ondary to off-label use of diuretics to combat the
"pooch" caused by hormones each month so as to
not miss a job.

"She'll be fine," Amma dismissed Bellamy's con-
cerns. "She is showing her age. However, getting
thinner really didn't help. We can airbrush anything these days, but I do so hate when my models
have those," she waved one many-ringed hand along
her face, "divets in their foreheads. Wrinkles is too
kind a word for those craters." She looked around,
seeming to finally notice the nurses at the rounded
counter at the end of the hallway watching them
as they spoke. "Anyhow. Her bad behavior made my
decision easy. She's done."

Bellamy stared hard at Amma, waiting for her to
pause, to soften, to take it back. Silence. Amma
pulled her phone out and glanced at it.

"Ah, Bellamy. Have you met my niece yet? She's
flying in from New York today and I really must go
change for dinner. After all, she's bringing Ammazing Models into the New York market. It's key that
she does not think one can cavort around looking
like..." Amma trailed off, gesturing at Bellamy's wrinkled pantsuit. "Especially as we merge the branches in two years...it simply won't do for my heir
apparent to get anything but my best. Not when
she and her sister will be running both markets in

tandem, eventually." Amma watched Bellamy with steady eyes, waiting for her barb to sink in.

Bellamy felt the floor dropping from beneath her heels. "I'm the heir apparent. I'm the next person who will be managing Ammazing Models." Bellamy couldn't stop the words from tumbling out, "You promised me this. You've said it several times." Most notably when she needed Bellamy to do something awful, like fire a model or work her seventh full-day shoot in a row.

"Oh Bellamy, really? Babe, you should know by now nothing ever matters in this business unless it's signed and witnessed. No contract? No deal. I knew you'd never have the spine to do what needs to be done. This moment right here was always going to happen. Losing clients. Caring about the models. They're not here to be your little sister, babe. They're here to work."

"Amma, I—I know this business better than any-one." Bellamy fought to keep her voice down, her anger rising as the ground steadied beneath her. "I know all of the models, the photographers, the client list. I know the most common shoot loca-tions. I've put in my time." Her voice continued to rise as she listed off the hard-earned knowledge she'd acquired through years of Amma's torment. "I've put in my time in front of and behind the camera."

"You know about *the* business, babe. You don't know about *business*. There's no room for heart here. What made you a good model herder was that the girls liked you. But now, you've become a liability. Calling an ambulance to set." Amma scoffed, waving her unlit Marlboro in Bellamy's face. "Really. She had a pulse. Your car would have been just fine." Amma placed the cigarette in her mouth and nodded, her heels clicking as she started toward the exit. She paused, pulling the filter from her mouth before saying over her shoulder, "You can expect your written letter of termination Friday. I'll pay you through then."

Chapter Two

Bellamy stared at the growing stack of mail on the small kitchen countertop in her cheap studio apartment. Turning her back on the pile, she slung open the door to the cream-colored fridge and let the cool air wash over her. A small, covered pot of leftover spaghetti waited forlornly beside a netted bag of tangerines and a mostly gone jug of oat milk.

"You are not cheering me up at all," she accused the sad groceries before easing the door closed and gathering her courage. The bills would need to be faced, there was no more putting it off. In the month and one week since Amma had fired her, Bellamy had sold the bulk of her designer clothes, applying to position after position at modeling agencies, film agencies, and even temp office jobs. No bites. It didn't help that her only consistent boss for the past decade remained unforgiving about the lost revenue from the bikini shoot and couldn't be used as a reference.

"Now or never," she muttered, digging out the fat envelope that she knew was her proposed lease renewal. Sliding a grown-out gel-manicured finger under the edge of the sealed flap, she took her time tearing the paper apart. With insurance rates rising, so were rent rates. Inside the dreaded envelope was what would essentially be the pathetic stamp of finality on her time in LA.

"Temporary stamp," she told herself firmly. "You'll come back. Just figure out some things ...like funding..." her voice trailed off when the typewritten words on the new lease option stared her in the face. "Like a lot of funding." Bellamy groaned, pushing her newly self-cut bangs off her forehead and letting the envelope drop to the floor. Where it could stay and rot for all the good it did her.

Envelope after envelope was either asking for money for bills or asking for money for charity. If she didn't cut her losses, she would be the one asking for help from some of these charities. After organizing them into stacks—one for simple bills like credit cards, one for bigger bills like her car payment and electricity, and one for the trash, Bellamy pulled the pot of spaghetti from the fridge and sat on the floor where her couch used to be. In her pocket, her phone buzzed.

Just got the all-clear from my doctor. It's official, we can date! Call me Mrs. Dr. Model, now! Bellamy snorted when she opened the text from Michaela.

Glad something good happened from that whole thing, Bellamy typed back with her thumb, twirling a fork in the cold noodles. *Any chance the hospital is hiring?* Bellamy paused, hovering her finger over the send button. She really didn't want to worry M about her job situation. Sure, the model had heard through the grapevine about Bellamy's firing, but Bellamy herself hadn't had the heart to give her the details. With some quick taps, she deleted the second part of the message, added a red heart, and pushed send.

"All right, Bellamy," she muttered to herself between bites, for once in her life not caring one iota about eating carbs two days in a row, "get a plan in place." Scrolling through social media while she ate wasn't helping at all. "Highlight reel, it's a highlight reel," she reminded herself softly, exiting the app and opening up her text list. Surely something in her recent texts would spark some ideas.

After scrolling past local friends that were in just as hard a place as her, and past models she'd been texting about call times as long as a month ago, Bellamy paused and scrolled back up. The last text from her mother had been a few days ago, a snap of her and Bellamy's stepfather leaning against the rails on the upper deck of a cruise ship. Bellamy had dropped them off at the port almost two months ago for their 101 day World Tour Cruise. It was the trip of a lifetime; one her mother had dreamed about for years. Bellamy enlarged the photo, taking in the happy smiles, the big straw hat shading her mother's face from the sun, and the cute little cocktail glass with an umbrella in her hand.

Hey Mom, I hope the cruise is going great! You look cute! Bellamy added a little kiss emoji and hit the send button. Her mom had retired from teaching less than a year ago, and she and her slightly older husband, Jonathan, had been planning their retirement adventures since they'd met and gotten married when Bellamy was still in high school.

Before Bellamy could click out of the text message, her phone began to buzz, and her older sister's photo and name popped up on the screen.

"What are you clairvoyant?" Bellamy greeted her.

"Hmm, are you thinking about how much nicer it would be to fly out to LA and get dropped off at a port to take a super long cruise and then come back home just in time for Christmas than it is to be a working adult? Because if you are...then yes, I am." Clare didn't bother with saying 'hi' either. "I'm surprised I caught you, you usually send me straight to voicemail this time of day."

"Oh, uh...yeah. Just an off-day. Not at a photo-shoot or anything." Bellamy dropped the fork into the now empty pot and laid back on the carpet, staring at the ceiling. "What's up?"

"Nothing big, just calling to see if Mom had checked in with you at her last port. She didn't send me a text so I was hoping she'd sent you one." Clare had long been the worrier in the family.

"Yeah, no, she did. It was a few days ago, right? They're like back out to sea or something for a while, I think."

"Mmm," Bellamy heard rustling through the phone, "let me find the itinerary she gave me." Somewhere in Clare's background, an oven timer was beeping, "Oh shoot! Hang on, let me call you back, that's the scones for the late-night Bingo and Beers."

Just like that, Clare was gone and Bellamy was left staring at the small spider slowly crawling across the ceiling of her soon to be too-expensive-to-stay-in old apartment, a silent phone in hand.

Bellamy knew at some point she'd have to tell her big sister about her job. She just hated always being the screw-up in the family. Clare ran an adorable bakery in Treeview, was married, and had a thirteen-year-old daughter. Their brother Adrien had played college ball, been in talks to play pro, but blew his knee his final championship game before graduation. Luckily, since he was somewhat of a hometown hero, he'd easily spun his miscellaneous business degree into a successful real estate company along the beautiful shores of Lake Michigan.

And then there was her. Baby Bellamy. The girl with dreams too big for home, who'd tried and tired, and failed and failed.

Before she could fall deeper into her self-pity spiral, her phone rang again. Bellamy didn't even look at the screen as she answered, "Mom's fine, I'm sure she'll check in with you in a few days."

"Miss Wilson?" A crisp, unfamiliar voice responded.

"Yes, yes this is Miss Wilson." Bellamy sat up straight, adopting her professional voice. Finally, a company was getting back to her to set up an interview!

"I'm Emily with Wilshire Sunset Apartments. I realize that your new lease has had quite a jump, and I wanted to call and verify that you will be either be signing it or giving your notice by the end of the week? We do require the 30-day notice, or we will have to charge you the month-to-month rate." The crisp voice lowered slightly, as if confiding in a close friend, "Believe me, you do not want to know what the month-to-month rate is. It's a significant advantage to sign the lease."

"Ah..." Bellamy pulled her phone from her ear and quickly flipped into the calendar there. "The end of the week is tomorrow."

"Yes, Miss Wilson, it is. That's why we're offering this courtesy call. If you need anything, please do not hesitate to contact me. We'll expect your lease to be dropped off at the office tomorrow."

"Thank you," Bellamy whispered as the phone disconnected. Her head sank into her hands and Bellamy pressed her palms hard against her mouth to suppress a scream of frustration. Spurred on by the timeline of tomorrow, Bellamy popped up to her feet, dropped the saucy pan in the sink, and grabbed the stack of small bills.

Dragging her last remaining designer bag across the counter, she fished out a pen, and using the back of the giant lease envelope, she listed out each pending bill. Then she grabbed the smaller stack, which was unfortunately filled with larger expenses, and made them their own list. With her trusty cellphone calculator, Bellamy totaled up the remainder of her car loan, her credit card bills, and her utilities. Then she opened up the bank app on her phone, held it up to her face, and waited for it to unlock.

The meager number staring back at her was enough to pay her utilities through November when her lease would end. It wasn't enough to pay rent for December. It wouldn't even cover December's car payment if she didn't get a job within the next few days.

Bellamy grabbed the lease and flipped to the contact page at the back. With slow, careful typing, she informed Emily with Wilshire Sunset Apartments that the email she was sending was to inform her, in writing, that she would not be renewing her lease, and would vacate the apartment no later than November twenty-seventh. The day before Thanksgiving.

Then, with shaking hands, she switched over to her contacts and called Clare.

"Bellamy! Hi there, so sorry I completely forgot to call you back. So you heard from Mom?"

Bellamy felt the tears building in the back of her throat, her eyes already starting to water, "Yeah, yeah, I did. Clare, I—"

"What's wrong?" All the cacophony behind Clare's voice when she first picked up the phone quieted, and Bellamy knew her sister had closed the big swinging door at the bakery to better hear her.

"I need to come home," she eked out in a tiny voice before the sobs began.

"Okay, sweetheart, okay."

The instant mothering in Clare's voice had the same effect it had always had on Bellamy when she was upset, and she sobbed harder at the gentle sympathy and genuine love.

When it became apparent Bellamy wasn't going to say more, Clare clarified, "Did you want to come home for Thanksgiving? Or maybe this weekend?"

"Maybe..maybe. I don't have a home anymore. I don't have a job. I'm all alone." Bellamy spilled the whole story out in a matter of minutes, explaining about Amma and the rising rent and her difficulty finding a job. When she'd finished and she was all cried out, she explained, "I just need to get back on my feet. I have so many good ideas. I know I can make it work. I just need some time. And some money."

"Okay, Belly Baby—"

"Don't call me that," Bellamy half laughed half sobbed.

"Sorry." Another timer went off in the background and Bellamy could hear Clare sliding a tray around on the oven racks. "Just old habit. Anyhow, you know what? That works great. You know how crazy it can be here for the holidays. I could really use the extra hand. We'll put you in Kevin's office...I know it's just a futon, but, well...it's free. Olivia will be so happy to have you home for the holidays. You know how much she misses you."

Bellamy nodded even though her older sister couldn't see her through the phone.

"So, you know. Perfect timing. Do you need money for a plane ticket?" Clare, Clare the Mother Bear was living up to her childhood nickname, as she always did.

"No." Bellamy thought about her car, the one she'd eyed for months before buying, now hanging like an albatross of payments from her neck. She should be able to sell it for enough to pay off the loan and get a ticket home easily enough. "No, I've got it."

"Okay, all right. It's about to be all right. Keep your chin up, and just let me know when to pick you up at the airport."

"Love you Clare, Clare the Mother Bear."

"Love you too, Belly Baby."

Chapter Three

Bellamy slid the airplane window open as the plane entered its final descent. Thankfully, the little hopper flight from the Detroit Metro airport to the Grand Bay View airport at the northern peak of the lower peninsula of Michigan had only two seats per row. After the six-hour flight in the middle seat between a bickering couple, Bellamy was grateful not just for the space, but for the relative peace and quiet as she watched the gorgeous blue-green waters of both Lake Michigan and Lake Huron appear. The dense pine forests were spotted with uniformly square farmlands for the last few miles before Treeview's roadways and businesses appeared.

While Treeview wasn't exactly a city, it was one of the larger towns in Northern Michigan. One side was fronted by beachfront bed and breakfasts, and one side was surrounded by a state forest. The other two sides, of course, were developed for housing and businesses.

In what felt like mere minutes the plane had bumped lightly to the ground and finished its taxi. The walk down the departure ramp felt end-less as Bellamy's stomach churned, both excited to see her sister and dreading the inevitable look of disappointment. Behind her, the small carry-on she dragged thunked across the threshold into the smoothly carpeted airport gate area. Bellamy straightened her shoulders and reminded herself that she was here to regroup and that the stay was temporary. In a few months, she'd return to LA and start her own modeling agency. After all, nothing would prove that she could be a success quite like, well, becoming one.

"Aunty Baa Baa!" A jubilant shout rang through the travelers filing through the security exit.

Bellamy's head snapped up at the nickname, a car-ryover from when her niece, at age two, had thought Bellamy's name was 'Bellamby'. With a grin, Bellamy stepped to the side and dropped her carry-on just in time to catch her sprinting niece in a great big hug, "Livvy! Oh my gosh, how did you get so tall?"

"I think it's called genetics," Clare answered dryly, waiting for her turn to hug Bellamy. "She looks an awful lot like her aunt did at that age."

Bellamy held Olivia at arm's length and took in her long gangly limbs, still awkward with all the growth happening. Then she grinned at Clare and teased, "Yes, already taller than her mother, I see." Despite being the oldest of the three Wilson siblings, at only five foot three, Clare had long been the shortest. "What was I, twelve, when I passed you?"

Clare rolled her eyes good naturedly as she pulled Bellamy into her own embrace, squeezing tightly for a long minute. "Yeah, I'm pretty sure I was eighteen because you tried to convince me you should be able to buy a Mega Millions ticket first, on the basis of height alone." She kissed Bellamy quickly on the cheek and asked, "How many checked bags did you bring?"

"Just one," Bellamy answered, waiting for the inevitable jokes about how impossible it had to be for her to travel so lightly, given her history of bringing home piles of outfits. To her surprise, no jokes came.

Olivia grabbed her hand and dragged her toward the baggage claim, singing, "I love you, a bushel and a peck!"

"A bushel and peck and a hug around the neck!" Bellamy joined her, choking back tears. For the first time in the past week, they were tears of happiness. She'd forgotten how good it felt to be with family.

Two hours later, after some last-minute shopping for the big dinner Clare was making tomorrow for Thanksgiving, they arrived at Clare and Kevin's house.

"Bellamy, I'm sure you're exhausted," Clare called over her shoulder as she stepped out of the driver's seat. "I made up the futon already, feel free to take a nap." She popped open the back of the vehicle, still talking. "I'm so sorry, I know you just got here, but I really need to get down to the bakery."

"She left Dad in charge," Olivia giggled like Kevin running the bakery was the biggest joke.

"Yes, I did." Clare checked her watch. "And right about now he should be getting ready to pull the bread from the proofer, so I need to get down there." Clare loaded her arms with grocery bags while Bellamy hefted her suitcase and carry-on from the open hatchback of the minivan.

Olivia held a hand up to her face and mock-whispered far too loud, "Last time he was supposed to do that he completely forgot because he got stuck in a work meeting and the bread ended up being like three times too big and you could barely even get the pans off the racks." She nodded, her hazel eyes wide for dramatic emphasis. "Anyhow, I gotta go work on my lines, and then Melly and me are going to make a video for PlayBox." Olivia grabbed the last grocery bag.

Clare sighed, "Fine, but you know the rules."

Olivia nodded, " 'No low-cut shirts, no tiny skirts, no identifying information like age or address'," she ticked off on her fingers, obviously used to quoting the social media rules. "See you after your nap, Aunty Baa Baa!" Olivia skipped away, housekey in hand.

Bellamy followed them up the steps of the front porch and into the cozy home. "Oh my gosh, you already decorated for Christmas?"

Clare looked around as she stepped out of her clogs, perplexed. "No, this is clearly Thanksgiving décor."

Bellamy took in the warm twinkling lights and the deep red maple leaf garland over the fireplace. "Oh, yeah. Okay." She raised a brow at the stuffed snowman sitting cheerily beside the wood rack. "Um, anyhow, I'm really not that tired, I can come help out at the bakery." She rubbed her arms, the short sleeves she'd left LA in just a bit too chilly for the brisk fall air, even indoors. "Besides, I came home to help, not to freeload." She offered a half smile, wrinkling her nose to make light of the situation.

Clare hesitated, then nodded decisively. "Okay. I have so many pie orders for tonight and tomorrow, it's not even funny. Let's get the cold stuff in the fridge," She raised her voice to call up the stairs after Olivia, "Olivia can put away the rest of the groceries later!"

A long pause and then a faint, "Yes, Mom, whatever," answered her.

Bellamy dragged her bags to the room off the entrance way, the door hidden to the left of the staircase, and gingerly opened it. Her brother-in-law's home office had been transformed into a temporary bedroom for her, with the futon pulled into a neatly made bed, two quilts folded at the foot of it. A fluffy towel set and her old high school hoodie also waited on the bed for her. "You're the best!" She called through the door to her sister, pulling the sweatshirt on. Normally, she'd want to look a little nicer her first time back in town for a few years, but she'd sold all her best outfits before leaving LA, and she had a sneaking suspicion that whatever she wore was going to end up dusted in flour anyhow.

"Okay, let's hustle," Clare stomped her feet back into her clogs, a single grocery bag now hanging from one wrist.

"Yes Clare, Clare, the Mother Bear," Bellamy said with a grin, sliding her bright pink sneakers back on. "Need me to carry anything?"

"We're good." And with that the sisters locked the door and trotted down the porch steps side by side.

Clare had taken the opportunity to list out the numbers and types of pies needed on the short drive to bakery, explaining to Bellamy the order of which ones to make first. The timing was pretty precise, because despite having a large commercial kitchen in the back of the little bakery, the sheer number of orders was going to require perfection.

As Clare pulled into the small employee parking lot at the back of the Main Street storefront, Bellamy shoved down her guilt. If she had some earlier, or maybe not come at all, then her sister would have had the whole morning to prep and bake.

"Does Alice still work here?" Bellamy thought of the sweet older woman who did the early morning donuts at Nothin' But Sugar, the cutesy name of Clare's bakery.

Clare's face softened for a moment, a small frown taking over the determined concentration that had been there, "No, sweetheart. She passed last February."

"Oh." Bellamy bit her lower lip, "I'm so sorry. I didn't know."

"Well, you've been really busy. That Amma woman had you working like a dog. I just didn't really have a good time to tell you. I couldn't leave it in a voicemail."

Bellamy nodded. There was nothing quite like being at rock bottom at twenty-eight and realizing how very many things she'd screwed up by trusting Amma. A fresh start would be good. One where she could really make something of herself, really prove that all the time and distance had been more than worth it.

"Yeah. I'll do better when I go back, Clare. Even when I'm busy, I'll answer the phone."

Clare beeped the van locked and led the way to the back entrance of the bakery, typing in the keycode to the door there and gesturing Bellamy through. "Okay, good." She didn't sound convinced.

Once inside, the yeasty smell of rising bread combined with the sugar scent of cakes and cookies was intense. Bellamy took a deep breath, inhaling the scent that was, for all of her childhood, the epitome of the holidays. "It smells amazing."

"It smells like Kevin took another business call at the wrong time," Clare grumbled as she set the grocery bag on a metal tabletop. Without hesitation, she hustled over to the proofing box and slung the door open, grabbing the top tray and sliding it gently onto the counter. She called to Bellamy as she grabbed the next tray, "Can you set the left two ovens to four-twenty-five, please? As soon as it dings, drop the temp down to three-fifty."

Bellamy nodded and walked over to the ovens on the left bank, hearing the internal fans whirl on as she turned the knobs. "Are they supposed to be this loud?"

"Hmm?" Clare looked over from where she was setting a fourth tray on the counter. "Oh, it's the steam convection. These babies were an investment, but well worth it."

Bellamy stepped back and looked around. In the three years since she'd been in the bakery, a lot had changed. "Whoa, you really did do a total renno in here, huh?"

"Just in the back. My goal is to update the customer area next year if we can afford it. I have about a quarter of what I'd need saved so far. But, luckily, this is the busiest time of the year, so we're likely to double that by year's end." Clare was now dusting the tops of the puffy loaves with flour. Then, she pulled a knife off the magnetic rack at the back of the counter and began slashing at the tops. Bellamy watched, fascinated, as Clare added a specific style to each loaf. Some were simple rectangles with diagonal cuts, and others were in more decorative circles or ovals with swirls or leafy patterns. "Can you go look for Kevin? He should be in the office, same place it always was."

"What about when the ovens ding?"

"I've got it. Let him know he can head home to keep an eye on Olivia since her friend Melanie should be there soon. Then you and I will get to work on the pies."

"On it!" Bellamy gently patted the ovens behind her as if to say goodbye and headed toward the office, really more of a closet, just off the swinging door that separated the kitchen from the customer area. It was empty.

Shrugging, Bellamy pushed through the swinging door just in time to watch a customer carrying a bakery box exit through the glass front door.

The man at the counter, about two inches too tall to be Kevin, turned, already saying, "Hey Clare, Kev asked me to step in for a few so he could meet somebody for a loan signing, he'll be—" He broke off when his green eyes met hers. "Bellamy?"

Bellamy blinked twice. Standing behind the counter of her older sister's bakery was her brother's best friend...and the first boy she'd ever loved.

Chapter Four

Acutely aware that she was un-showered, jet-lagged, and wearing her baggy decade-old high school hoodie, Bellamy shifted her weight from foot to foot, tucking her hands into the front pocket of said hoodie to avoid habitually pushing her bangs back.

"Oh, um, yeah...I....Hi, Luke. What are you doing here?" She slowly inched away from the door entering the space behind the counter.

"As I thought I was telling Clare," Luke winked, the confidence he'd always had was having the same flip-flopping effect on Bellamy's stomach as it had when he was a senior in high school and she was a freshman, "Kev had to step out, so I'm just covering for a few. I think the better question is the reversal: What are you doing here?" He leaned casually against the counter. The green and blue flannel shirt he wore was just soft enough and just tight enough to show off the outline of his biceps.

Oh boy, some things never changed. Bellamy removed her gaze from his body with effort, her mouth suddenly dry. "Oh, you know...just here for the holidays." She forced a small grin. "How's Alice?"

Luke's posture stiffened for a moment before he shrugged, turning to look at the cupcakes and drumming his fingers on the glass display. "You'd have to ask her. Last I heard, New York was treating her well."

"Oh—" Bellamy wasn't sure how to respond, but luckily, she was saved by the perfectly timed arrival of her golden-retriever-esque brother-in-law.

"Bellamy! Or should I say Aunty Baa Baa?" Kevin breezed into the bakery, the bells over the door still jingling merrily as he swept Bellamy up in a hug, kissed her cheek, and then immediately turned to shake Luke's hand. "Thanks for the pinch-hitting, man. We just really wanted to get the closing completed before the holidays for this family." He turned to Bellamy, "Does Adrien know you made it in yet?"

Kevin worked as a mortgage broker, which often ended up with him working closely with Adrien's real estate team. A near genius at numbers, Kevin was not just well-liked, but well-respected by all the local credit unions and banks.

"I guess so?" Bellamy realized she'd left her cell phone in her carry-on back at Clare's house. It was oddly freeing to not be chained to it, waiting for barking orders from Amma, or the inevitable crisis at a photoshoot.

"Hey, look, good to see ya Bells, I gotta head back over to the shop." Luke lifted one hand in farewell and disappeared into the afternoon sun, loping quickly down the sidewalk and out of sight.

"Clare said that you can head home to stay with Olivia and her friend Michelle," Bellamy said absently, staring after Luke.

"Michelle?" Kevin fished his car keys back out of the pocket of his suit jacket. "You mean Melanie? Got it. Oh shi—"

"You forgot my bread again," Clare stood at the door to the kitchen, holding a wooden spoon and tapping it against the opposite hand like some old-timey gangster. "And I know you weren't about the swear in my bakery. Nothin' but Sugar, Honey, you know the rules." She broke into a small smile as Kevin picked her up and spun her around, planting a big showy kiss on her lips before murmuring something only Clare could hear.

Bellamy turned away, feeling a bit like an onlooker. The way Kevin adored Clare hadn't changed at all since they'd started dating when they were both attending the local community college. At only fourteen, Bellamy had thought they were so gross..and so cute. At twenty-eight, she still felt just about the same, if not a little bit envious of the happily ever after her older sister had created.

"Okay," Clare waved the spoon in the air like an old war general rallying her charges. "Kevin, you're home with the girls. They're making a promo video for social media for their play, keep an eye on them, *please*." She turned and pointed the spoon at Bellamy, "And you, dearest sister, are officially my minion for the rest of the afternoon and evening. Pies, pies, pies! Hop to!"

Three hours later, Bellamy's shoulders were aching from rolling out dough and sliding around laden oven trays from the waiting rack to the ovens, to the cooling rack. She had to hand it to her sister, though. Clare was efficient, tireless, and her timeline was on point. The bakery was filled with the aromas of cinnamon, nutmeg, caramels, and roasting pecans.

"Nice work!" Clare held up one floury hand from where she was carefully latticing the tops of a row of apple pies, waiting for a high five.

With a snort, Bellamy slapped the offered palm and sank against the edge of the long, in-set cutting board they were working at. "Nobody does that anymore, you know."

"What, lattices? It's a classic."

"No, high fives."

"What? Also a classic!" Clare was focused again on creating the patterned crust, deftly weaving the dough strips.

"It's just about pick-up time for the evening order." Bellamy watched the minute hand ticking closer to the twelve at the top of the large clock over the sink. "Want me to stay with the ovens for the timers, or do the register?"

"I think it's best if I keep working here, I'm in the zone. The list is tucked under the register, just flick the light switch on the door sign to signal we're ready for pick-ups and they should start coming in for their two-hour window." She tilted her head toward the stack of pie boxes Bellamy had unfolded and labeled earlier. "Can you start getting pies boxed up for the next few minutes?"

"On it!" Even though the work was tiring, and she was really starting to feel the jetlag, Bellamy was enjoying the time with her big sister. Clare had caught her up on the local happenings while they'd worked. There were a lot of holiday events in Treeview that they'd be baking for. Including the play Olivia was currently studying lines for. Or maybe making a social media video. Bellamy doubted the thirteen-year-old's timeline was as precise as Clare's.

"Pecan, Dutch apple, or pumpkin first?"

"Ah, let's do the Dutch apple, then the pecan, I'd prefer for the custard to set longer on the pumpkin before jostling it too much."

Bellamy nodded and slid out the boxes labeled for the Dutch apple pies, arranging them in front of the cooling rack. "So, Olivia has social media now?"

Clare sighed heavily, her hands speeding up as if to convey her frustration. "Yes. It wasn't my preference, but all her friends have it, and Kevin hated that she was being left out of things because we didn't let her."

"But does she even need a cellphone? We didn't have them until we could drive." Bellamy eased a heavy pie into the box, inhaling the sweet and tart apple smell, the cinnamon undertone a delight. "I mean, I'm just saying, that would solve the whole thing."

"No, Bellamy, it wouldn't. Trust me, it's a lot more complicated than that. Anyhow, she has to follow the rules, and I have her passwords so I can check in on it anytime I want to." Clare pushed the pie she'd finished to the side, sliding it hard enough it bumped into the previous pie with a thunk. "Look, it's nuanced."

Bellamy nodded, pressing her lips together. Clare had long said she didn't want to allow social media use at all for Olivia. Gingerly, Bellamy added, "Hey, sorry. I just know how you felt about it and...anyhow, how can I have your back? Want me to like add her on mine so I can watch what she's doing?"

Clare grunted out a half groan half laugh, "Oh you sweet naive Aunt. Kids have layered accounts where they make sure parents see only what they want. You're cool, and she's absolutely into this play thing because she wants to be just like you, but I don't think even movie star Aunt Bellamy is hip enough to get the friend's account."

Bellamy wrinkled her nose, "As if being a background extra several times and having one non-speaking role counts as being a movie star. Anyhow, okay, yeah. Probably not then."

Clare grabbed the next ball of dough to roll out from the walk-in cooler, gently bumping Bellamy with her hip as she passed. "Hey. I know you're just getting caught up and want to help. But it's okay to leave the parenting to the parents and just be the fun aunt. Besides, I check her DMs regularly and there's nothing there but emoji's and sharing little video clips. It's honestly pretty nerdy, and I'm at least happy about that."

After easing the last Dutch apple pie from the cooling rack into a box, Bellamy began taping them closed, pressing her lips together to stop herself from asking how they'd know if Olivia had other secret social media accounts. After all, Clare was right, she wasn't the parent. And they probably had a system. "So, tell me about this play anyhow. Livvy's acting in it?"

Clare nodded, her rolling pin work becoming less aggressive by the moment. "Yeah, she's got a speaking role, but she's also helping with costuming. Her and Melanie both decided to do it."

"That's pretty cool, are they like thrifting for the costumes, or are they using some from the old basement closet?" Bellamy had spent a lot of hours after school when she was a freshman helping sort and label the costumes in the school's storage while waiting for Adrien to finish football practice.

"Oh, it isn't a school production, although she has been interested in joining drama club once she's in high school. It's at The Pine."

"That newer community theater you were telling me they were fundraising for a few years ago?" Bellamy finished taping the boxes closed.

"That's the one. If you're still in town in a few weeks—"

"I'm sure I will be." Bellamy winced.

"—Then you'll have to go and watch it, of course. They're doing A *Christmas Carol* and opening night is the same weekend as Christmas in the Town-square, so the timing's not great, but I know Olivia will love to have you there."

"I'm there. Definitely." Bellamy was happy they'd gotten back their equilibrium after her over-step. Which reminded her of another uncomfortable moment where she'd seemed to over-step.

"Pecan next?"

Clare nodded, using a spatula to scrape her apple, golden raisin, and warming spice filling into the next pie crust. "Yes, please."

As Bellamy lined up the first row of pecan pie boxes, she asked over her shoulder, hoping to sound casual, "So, when did Alice move to New York?"

"Alice?" Clare set the bowl aside, wiping her hands on her apron and cocking her head to the side. "Oh you mean Luke's Alice?" She paused, casting a narrow-eyed look over her shoulder. "Any particular reason you're asking? Maybe because you loooove him?" Clare teased.

"Oh, stop! That's so silly, I was a kid back then." Bellamy purposefully turned to the cooling rack to grab a pie so her sister wouldn't see the blush warming her cheeks.

"Well, I can't think of any other reason than that, considering you've met Alice all of...twice?"

"She seemed nice," Bellamy offered lamely, nestling the pie into the box and turning for the next. "Besides, I thought they were about to get engaged?"

"Yeah, he had the ring and everything."

"I know, you told me that part!"

"Oooh that's right, we video-called last Christmas, right after dinner."

"Yeah, yeah, he showed the ring to Adrien right before they left, while she was in the bathroom, and Adrien was being such a punk about losing his wingman."

Clare chuckled, "Yes! I remember that whole call now." Her laughter faded and she shrugged before finally answering, "She got a job and just couldn't turn it down. They tried the distance for a bit but...well, I don't have to tell you how hard it is to juggle a highly demanding job and long-distance loved ones."

A flash of guilt churned in Bellamy's chest. "Yeah. I can't believe how much I've missed here. I feel like I know half of every story."

Clare ran the spinning dough cutter through her next rolled-out rectangle as she said simply, "It's okay, Belly Baby. You're here now, and you get to make some of those stories with us." Then she dusted her hands on her apron and looked up at the clock. "Now, you, to the register. Any maybe...put on an apron?" She said, eyeing Bellamy's flour and apple-filling-covered sweatshirt with amusement.

Chapter Five

"Aunty Baa Baa! Wakey, wakey!"

Bellamy groaned. "What time is it?"

"Four-thirty in the morning." Olivia giggled, giving Bellamy's shoulder another enthusiastic shake.

"Why are you torturing me? You're a teenager, you're supposed to sleep in until noon and get mad at me when I wake *you* up." Bellamy grudgingly slid into a sitting position, shoving the quilts to the foot of the futon.

"It's tradition." Olivia pranced out of the room, flicking the overhead light on as she went. "Mom said to be ready to go in fifteen," she called over her shoulder before shutting the door.

"Ugh," Bellamy responded. She really didn't know how Clare, who was eight years older than her, was intentionally getting up with fewer than five hours of sleep. It had been well past ten when they'd locked up Nothin' But Sugar and headed home. Practically a zombie by then, Bellamy hadn't bothered to unpack more than a large tee-shirt to sleep in before falling onto the futon.

Now, she scrambled through her luggage to find a pair of jeans and a long-sleeved waffle-knit that fit so perfectly you'd never guess she'd gotten from the bargain bin.

A knock on the door interrupted her hunt for her toothbrush. "Bellamy, hustle-up!" Clare called through the door.

"I am, I am!" Bellamy snagged the toothbrush from the bag and dashed through the house to the downstairs bathroom. "Your floors are freezing!" She called, instantly regretting not hunting for a pair of socks.

Whatever Clare said in response was lost to the sound of the water running. Bellamy rinsed, brushed, and rinsed quickly. Eying her wild hair in the mirror, Bellamy tried a loose, tousled look. "Nope," she muttered to herself as she yanked her light brown tresses into a high ponytail. As an afterthought, she snagged two sparkling bobby pins with little snowflakes at the ends from the ledge by the mirror to pin back her bangs. "Good enough," she told herself, swiping ineffectually at the smudged mascara under her eyes. "I've heard the raccoon look is in this year, anyhow." Then, raising her voice she called, "I'm ready! Just gotta get socks and shoes."

"I've got a pair of socks for you Auny Baa Baa, they're extra cozy." Olivia waited by the backdoor, fully dressed and wearing a puffy vest over her own long-sleeved shirt.

"Thanks, Livvy."

Within minutes the three women were out of the house and on their way to the bakery.

"Hey, what's Kev do every year when you two get up before the chickens?" She turned to look at her niece in the backseat. "And whatever happened to child labor laws?"

"He's getting the turkey ready," Olivia answered.

At the same time, Clare said, "It's only child labor if she gets paid. This is mother-daughter bonding that happens to take place in a family-owned business."

"Ah, my mistake." Bellamy winked at Olivia before turning back around as Clare parked the van behind the bakery in her usual spot.

Bellamy could see her breath in the air as she trudged behind her sister, grateful that soon the heating ovens of the bakery would mitigate the pre-dawn chill.

"Pick-ups start at nine, and since most of the pies we made yesterday are for those orders, I'll have both of you up in the front starting then. Bellamy, you'll run the till, Olivia you'll do the checklist and the handovers. Until then, we've got about fifteen coffee cakes, a dozen par-baked rolls, and a few take-and-bake pies to prep."

"Plus the extras," Olivia nodded sagely as she grabbed an apron from the drawer beside the sink. She tossed one to each woman before donning her own. "The extras are my favorite part; they're really the tradition."

Four long hours, and not a few flour smudges on her apron later, Bellamy flipped the on switch for the neon open sign.

"What's the list looking like?" Bellamy returned behind the counter and stood next to her niece to look over the clipboard.

"You guys did pretty well last night, compared to last year," Olivia stuck the pen back in the metal clip and ran a finger down the typed-out pre-order list. "I think it will be an early rush." She set the clipboard aside and propped her elbows on the glass show-case top, settling her chin in her hands, and turned to Bellamy. "Did Mom tell you about my play?"

"She did," Bellamy mirrored her pose as she answered, "I heard you're pulling double duty."

"I am." Olivia shrugged and added, "But I like it. Since I'm too young for the adult roles and too old to play Tiny Tim there's not many lines for me. But I do get to be a couple different townsfolk and one of Tiny Tim's siblings, so I do have some. Plus, the costuming is super cool."

"Are you doing more of a modern interpretation, or keeping it classic?" Bellamy eyed a car slowing down as it approached the street parking in front of Nothin' But Sugar.

"Classic. Which means Miss Everly—she's the costumer that's letting us intern with her—is teaching Melly and me about the types of clothes as we're making them. Which is like nerdy, but cool nerdy."

The sedan out front finished parking. Their first customer was right on time.

"You're making them? As in sewing them?" When Olivia nodded Bellamy raised her eyebrows. "Livvy, that's super cool. Isn't that a lot of work, though?"

"It is. Like, totally hard. We're a little behind, but Miss Everly says we can catch up if we don't get discouraged." Olivia waved as the door bells jingled. "Hi, Mrs. Patts." She skimmed the list, making a few checks with the pen. "Two pecan, one pumpkin, and one raspberry cheesecake coffee cake, right?"

"Hi Oliva, yes, absolutely right, dear." Mrs. Patts finished fishing in her purse as she approached the register, where Bellamy now waited. "Oh, as I live and breathe! Is that Bellamy Wilson? When did you get into town? So good to see you dear."

"Thank you, Mrs. Patts. Just here for the holidays," Bellamy gave what would be her stock answer as she rang in the order. "That will be forty-six dollars even, please."

Mrs. Patts handed over a stack of cash that she must have pre-counted and then slipped an envelope across the glass to Oliva. "That's for the extras, dear."

"Thank you, Mrs. Patts!" Olivia slid the envelope behind the list and clipped it onto the clipboard.

"Well, have to hustle. I've gotta get to the Family Grocery before they run out of whipped cream. Adam forgot it yesterday. Men!" She huffed airily, waving as she left. "Good to see you girls."

The next few pickups went about the same. Some customers were new faces that Bellamy hadn't met before, but most asked when she'd gotten into town. More than a few of the locals slid an envelope across the counter to Olivia, with the same message about it being 'for the extras.'

When there was finally a lull, Bellamy asked her niece, "Livvy, you have to tell me. What is going on with the mysterious envelopes?"

Olivia grinned and flipped the list off the top of the clipboard to reveal her growing stash. "Well, you know the stuff Mom's making in the back right now?

The stuff we did after finishing the rolls and coffee cakes and the pies for the orders?"

Bellamy nodded and gestured for her to continue.

"Now she's doing the *extra* extras."

"Right I got that. The stuff she donates to the community center meal. She's been doing that forever, but there were never any envelopes involved."

Olivia's face was practically glowing with joy. "That's because last year Uncle Adrien mentioned it in a business profile for the Made in Michigan journal, and then all the sudden some of the regulars brought in envelopes on Thanksgiving. Just to you know...help. Since Mom does it with no profit. So, now we get to give even more, which is the best."

Bellamy shook her head, some of the tiredness inside her washed away by the sense of community. "That's really something."

"Right? I think it's good. I think mostly people want to help, but they don't always know how. That's what Mom says, anyhow. Uncle Adrien just sort of gave an easy way for them to do it."

"Have I ever told you how wise you are for a teenager?"

"Oh my gosh Aunty Baa Baa, you're, like, so stuck on my being a teenager. Get over it!" Olivia rolled her eyes, as if to prove how much of a teen she was.

The wind picked up outside, and even with the door closed, Bellamy shivered from the draft. "Brr.

It sure got cold last night." She scooted from behind the counter to check to be sure the windows were all closed.

"It's November, it's supposed to be cold," Olivia said dryly, typing on her phone, now.

Bellamy rubbed her arms briskly, finishing her lap around the room. No open windows, it was just very drafty in the front of the bakery.

"Heyo!" The door swung open, accompanied by the cheerful jangle of the bells, and before Bellamy could even respond, her older brother was spinning her around in a big hug. "There's my baby sister. You get into town and don't even stop by to see your big brother in the first twenty-four hours?"

"It hasn't even been twenty-four hours, Adrien. Besides, out of the two of us, you're the one with a vehicle...so good work getting here." She grinned up at him when he set her back down.

"Well, guilty as charged. Happy to see ya, Sis, but I gotta admit I'm here on an errand."

"Ah, the truth, it stings so," Bellamy teased. "Whatcha up to?"

"Catch, Uncle Adrien!" Olivia tossed two loaves of bread, one right after the other, from behind the counter.

He caught them deftly, barely even looking.

"Show-off," Bellamy smirked.

"Rascal," Adrien returned. "Here to get the bread for Kev to stuff the bird." The wind outside howled, sending leaves tumbling down the street. "Sheesh, it's cold in here. Hang on, I got some of that heat wrap in my jeep, meant to get it up in here before now, but guess better late than never."

Adrien held the door for another customer as he jogged back out to his vehicle, loaves tucked in the crook of one elbow like a football.

"Oh, Bellamy!" A squeal, followed by the startled yowl of a small baby had Bellamy spinning around from her walk to the register.

"Julieann? Oh my gosh, and you have a baby?" Bellamy gave her old friend a quick half-hug and pulled back to look at the drowsy infant, snuggled into his mother's partially zipped coat and wrapped in a fluffy blanket.

"Yep." The shorter woman grinned and held out her free hand, a small diamond glittering there. "Andrew and I got married 'bout two years ago, and little Brian here is our first."

"Well, you are glowing. It's so nice to see you!" Bellamy gushed, thinking back to all the times they'd played MASH in middle school, and how Julieann had never put less than 3 kids in any of her spots.

"I can't believe you're here. You know, my mom still has that perfume ad you were in taped to her fridge." She giggled and added, "It may or may not be right next to that photo of our cast of *Our Town.*"

Bellamy felt her cheeks heat a little at the idea of Julieann's church pianist mother having a photo of her modeling for perfume...in a bikini...on her fridge for years. "Oh gosh, that's so sweet of her." She shook her head. "Feels like ages ago." The ad for *California Coast* had been the only national-level ad she'd been in, with most of her work being local, low-paying jobs. Just enough to get by on while still going to casting calls and auditions. Everything in LA was competitive.

"Well, we all thought it was pretty amazing. Our Bellamy, a model and on TV, all in the same year—you were practically the talk of the town." The baby in her arms started mewling quietly, turning his head and nuzzling into Julieann. "Ah, this little angel is getting hungry. Whoops! Guess I better get my order and get him on home."

Bellamy quickly cashed her out and Olivia offered to carry the pies to her car, so she didn't have to worry about tilting them in their boxes.

"So good to see you," Bellamy called as Adrien held the door again.

"Cute baby, huh?" Adrien set a roll of clear plastic on the wrought iron café table near the windows. "I helped her and Andrew get their house just after they got married. It's just down the road from

Mom's, you should think about stopping by, maybe bring a baby gift."

"Adrien," Bellamy narrowed her eyes at her brother and added, "I'm not a kid, you don't need to try to make me popular anymore. I don't even live here." Bellamy went on the offense, wondering how much Clare had or hadn't told their brother about her financial situation.

Adrien held up his hands in front of him, "All right, all right, I wasn't trying to get your hackles up. Just thought it might be nice. You two used to be so close. Might not hurt to rekindle some friendships if you're going to be here more than a weekend, is all."

"Ugh. Clare told you."

"Not the details, just the broad strokes. Nothin' to be mad about, Bellamy, no shame in things not working out."

"I don't want to talk about it," she said quickly as Olivia pranced back through the door. "Not here."

"If you're not into talking, come over here and help your big brother winterize the windows real fast."

It didn't take long for Adrien to remind Bellamy of how the insulating plastic worked. While their mother had always used a kit with the adhesive attached to pre-cut sheets, the separate kit pieces were just as easy. In no time, they had smaller windows taped up. With Olivia aiming the old hair dryer in Adrien's kit to tighten the plastic behind them, it was quick work.

"Okay, nice job, ladies. Now, this one's the doozy." The corner of Adrien's tongue was poking out of the side of his mouth as he studied the big storefront window.

"Do we need to do this one?" Bellamy asked.

"Well, Clare's been eating that heat bill for a few years now, and last year it helped a lot. Last I heard she's plannin' on replacing the windows as part of the redesign in here." He nodded to himself, rolling out the sheeting across the glass countertop. "This'll do it. She's been putting in a lot of extra hours this season, and if spending a few extra minutes getting this right will help...well, least we can do, right?"

"Right." Bellamy nodded. Back behind the counter again, Olivia was reabsorbed in her phone, completely oblivious.

Bellamy dragged one of the old chairs from beside the café tables over to the window as Adrien cut the large piece of plastic. She clambered onto the rickety chair, bracing her hand against the wall to stop the wobbling.

"Here, stick the adhesive on first, make sure you get it above the framing." Adrien tossed the roll of double-sided tape in a perfect throw, then turned to measure and cut the next section of sheeting.

As Bellamy reached above her head, the chair still wobbling, something outside the window caught her eye. There, standing on the sidewalk right in front of her, was Luke. He waved and mouthed something to her. She couldn't hear it through the glass, so she just smiled and waved, catching herself on the wall just before falling again.

Luke shook his head, his brows furrowing under his knit cap. He held up a finger and then jogged back across the street.

Bellamy watched him lower the tailgate of the dark blue pickup parked behind Adrien's jeep and slide a small ladder out.

"Ooh, that's what he was asking." She smiled and gave him a thumbs-up, almost losing her balance for the third time.

She hopped from the wobbly chair and darted to hold the door open for him. Behind him came another customer, and there was another vehicle in the process of parallel parking.

"Hey Bells, good to see you again." He and Adrien exchanged nods as he set up the ladder in front of the window.

"Hi, Luke. Thanks for, um, saving me from the wobbly chair."

"I gotcha, no biggie."

Adrien carried over the next sheet of plastic and they bumped fists, "Heard about Dale and Lola's. That where you're headed?"

Bellamy glanced down and noted the work boots and leather chaps Luke had on over his jeans. Which just so happened to frame his butt perfectly, as if to intentionally draw a wandering eye. It certainly drew hers, at least.

"Yeah, Lola's pretty distraught, with Dale's back still in recovery, and since I gotta cut the tree before I can clear it from the drive, she asked if I could grab her order on my way over; she was afraid she'd miss the pickup window."

"Excuse me, can I do my pickup now?" The older lady who had entered behind Luke now stood at the counter.

Bellamy cleared her throat, hoping nobody had noticed where her attention had been, feeling her cheeks heat.

Olivia dropped her phone on the display case with a clatter and picked up the clipboard. "Yes! Name, please?"

"Jenkins, should be two apple pies."

Bellamy scooted back behind the counter, pushing Adrien's pile of supplies to one side, and offered the grumpy woman a big smile. "So sorry about that, we're just doing some winterizing."

"Strange time to do that. Should have done it weeks ago. It is a bit too nippy out today. Heard there might be some snow." The woman tapped her cash on the counter while Olivia located her order on the list, and then brought the pies over.

"Twenty-eight, twelve, please." Bellamy rang her up, gave her, her change, and then greeted the next customer in line.

Six customers later, the bakery was already feeling warmer, and Bellamy found herself smiling up into Luke's green eyes as he stepped forward. "Nice work on the windows," She nodded to the now fully sealed storefront window and waved to Adrien as he held up a hand on his way out the door.

"See you guys tonight. Thanks for the hand, Luke."

"Easy day. Hey, can I get the order for Lola Envers? I know I'm not her designated pickup person, but they had a tree fall across the drive so..."

"I think we can trust you," Bellamy teased, "Afterall, we know where you're going to be eating dinner tonight. And there will be plenty of pie."

Clare always hosted a big dinner, and Luke's family had been joining their family for Thanksgiving even back when dinners were hosted by Bellamy's mom.

Olivia was back on her phone. Bellamy cleared her throat, and the teen looked up with a guilty smile. "Whoops, sorry. It's just that we got, like, thirty likes on our video already, and that's a lot for me and Melly. What was I supposed to be doing?"

"Can you grab the order for Lola Envers, please?"

Olivia nodded and made some checks on the list. "Oh, she prepaid; that's perfect, Uncle Luke! I'll get it from the back."

In the moment of silence while Olivia was getting another stack of pumpkin pies, Bellamy debated if she should say anything about her faux pas yesterday. Would it be better or worse to bring up Alice again? Maybe she should apologize, because it was starting to feel awkward.

"Look, Luke I'm—" She started.

Just as he said, "Hey, Bells, just a head's up my parents won't be at the dinner tonight. They're in Colorado with Lucy and Gia. So, ya know, just in case you were expecting to see them."

"Oh...yeah, thanks. Mine're on their cruise, so I guess that's four less."

"Heard they're having a blast. What was it you were going to say? Didn't mean to cut you off."

"I...oh," she waved a hand as she sputtered, "nothing, nothing at all."

"Here ya go!" Olivia slid the pumpkin pie across the counter to Luke.

"Thanks, kid. See ya tonight, Bells." He nodded and headed back out, another customer coming in after him.

The next two hours at the bakery flew. With only fifteen minutes left until the close of the pickup time, noon, they had only one customer left unchecked on the list.

"Do you know who Andrea Valentine is?" Bellamy tapped the pen absently against the clipboard as Olivia started loading loaves of unsold bread into reusable bags.

"Uh...her name is familiar. I think she's like on TV or something. Maybe the weather lady?" Olivia was setting one full bag on the counter when Clare could be heard calling for her from the kitchen. "Oh, it's time to box the pies for the community center. I'm sure she'll be here soon. If not, Mom's got her number on the receipt, I'm sure."

Having worked a few seasonal retail jobs in the past, Bellamy knew they'd need to tally the till before they could leave. Might as well do it while waiting; it would be easy enough to add Andrea Valentine's total in.

She'd just finished counting the paper money, but not the coins, when a woman in a purple suit dress burst through the door, her heels clicking. She seemed utterly impervious to the cold, with her highlighted blond hair falling in waves down her back, un-flattened by a hat.

"Clare?" The woman asked before looking up, pulling a paper out of her large purse along with her wallet.

"Ah, no, I'm her sister. But I can get her for you, Miss...?"

"Valentine," She set the paper and her wallet on the countertop, holding out her hand, "Andrea Valentine."

"Oh, you're our last order. I can help you. Unless you needed Clare for something special, she's right in the back."

"If you wouldn't mind. Here, go ahead and ring me up first." Bellamy fought down envy at the perfect manicure she displayed as she held out her platinum credit card.

"Sure thing." Andrea really did look familiar, even to her. After checking off the list, Bellamy ducked into the kitchen and asked Clare to come out to give Andrea her pies.

Clare gave Bellamy a look, but was out and wiping her hands on a clean dish towel within the time it took Bellamy to complete the credit card transaction.

"Andrea, so lovely to see you. How can I help?" Clare had her most professionally bland smile on, and it was only then that it clicked for Bellamy. An-

drea Valentine had been in Clare's class throughout school. She'd been spoiled, gorgeous, and the
prom queen. She was also from one of the most
wealthy families in Mackinac Bridge region, with
her father owning several TV and radio stations
in addition to his grandfather having been part of
the early motor city projects.

"Actually, Clare, I was hoping maybe I could
help you. I've always loved your cute little bakery,
and the minute my father announced this, I just
knew you would be perfect for it." Andrea held out
the glossy paper as if presenting a golden ticket.

"Oh." Clare gingerly took the flyer. "Thanks."

"Anyhow, read up on it, text me if you have
questions! Or, well, you can DM me on my socials
and I promise I'll accept." She scooped up the pie
and coffeecake boxes from the counter, the scent
of very expensive perfume wafting behind her as
she spun to leave. "Happy holidays!"

Bellamy raised her eyebrows, staring after the
local golden girl. "Wow. She really hasn't lost her
head-cheerleader enthusiasm, has she?"

"No," Clare answered slowly, still reading the
flyer. "But for once, Andrea Valentine's love of
flashing around her family's money might work in
our favor. How're your drawing skills?"

"About the same, I did tons of mockups and sketches for the photoshoots, why?" Bellamy leaned over her sister's shoulder and read:

COOKIES, CAKES, AND BREADS! WHO IS THE BEST ALL-AROUND BAKER IN THE TRI-COUNTY AREA?

WHO: Local bakers only.

WHERE: Treeview, Trout Bay, and Thistle Creek (BOTH home and business addresses must be within these county limits)

WHAT: Festival contest to be judged on live TV before the Christmas in Townsquare tree lighting ceremony. Friday, December 21st, 4:30 pm.

THE PRIZE: First place winner: $250,000 cash prize. Second place winner: $100,000.00 cash prize. Third place winner: $50,000.00 cash prize.

Details online, read all fine print. Prize winners will be obligated to participate in three charity events throughout the following calendar year.

"Whoa," Bellamy breathed, "that's a lot of cash."

"That's a whole renovation for the front of house here...and some really good seed money for your triumphant return to LA." Clare folded the paper.

"Well, if we won. We'll look at the details later tonight and take it from there. Right now, we have a highly anticipated delivery to make."

Throughout the next hour as Clare, Bellamy, and Olivia loaded and unloaded the minivan, Bellamy could not stop thinking about that prize money. It was her ticket back to LA. Whatever the rules were, she would do everything she could to help her sister win.

Chapter Six

The alarm on Bellamy's phone chirped to life with a jaunty instrumental song. Groaning, she shoved herself into sitting up on the futon for the second time that day. Once they'd completed the deliveries, Bellamy, Clare, and Olivia each went separate ways to crash for a well-earned nap while Kevin and Adrien alternated between standing outside by the grill, where the turkey was roasting, and watching the game on TV.

With a yawn, Bellamy stumbled to her bag and pulled out the gallon-sized Ziploc that held her bottles of shampoo and conditioner, facewash, and lotions. Feeling more zombie-like than human, she staggered past the living room and into the bathroom, locking the door behind her.

"Bless you, Clare, Clare the Mother Bear," she offered quietly to the empty room when she saw the fluffy folded towel and washcloth on the corner of the sink vanity.

The hot shower felt especially delightful, but Bellamy recalled from experience that stepping out of the steamy bathroom would be a shock, especially with wet hair. Still, she thought as she washed, the small creature comforts of a clean head of hair were not to be denied.

Out of the shower, she wrapped her hair up in the towel and set to work. Working in the small patch of mirror she'd swiped the steam off of, Bellamy finally removed the old mascara from under her eyes. After layering on two different eye creams, she decided to give her skin a breather and leave off the foundation. The importance of having make-up-free days was something she'd talked a lot about with the more experienced models when she'd first started out. It was probably the best advice she'd been given, really.

A few dabs of sparkling amber eyeshadow and two layers of mascara later, she was dashing back to her temporary bedroom with the towel wrapped tightly around her body. Thankfully, no guests had arrived yet.

Since nobody had yet knocked on either door to get her attention, Bellamy took the time to unpack her bags, draping some items over the back of Kevin's desk chair, and stacking the folded clothes on the seat of the chair. The red sequined mini dress she put on the top of the chair stack was the last truly high-end designer item she'd kept. That dress and the matching satin heels were the most expensive things she owned now.

"Temporary. It's only temporary," she whispered to herself. It wasn't so much that she had hated parting with the designer clothes, but more the shame of being twenty-eight and owning, essentially, nothing. Giving the designer dress one last gentle pat, she dug out a more practical leggings and sweater dress combination. She added a thin pair of patterned socks and expertly wove her wet hair into a French braid.

The living room was still empty when she exited the office, and a quick glance through the glass sliding door wall showed her that Olivia and the guys were outside by the grill. No sign of Clare. Bellamy turned and trotted up the stairs.

"Clare! You up here?"

"Yep, just finishing getting dressed. Come on in," Clare called from the master bedroom at the end of the hall.

Bellamy stepped into the room just as Clare's head popped through the neck of the cable knit sweater she was pulling on. "How're you feeling? I don't know how you're awake, let alone ready to host Thanksgiving dinner."

Clare waved her off, selecting a pair of earrings from the glass dish on her dresser. "Oh please, nothing being a mom hasn't prepared me for, honestly."

Bellamy plopped on the foot of Clare's bed, folding her legs into criss-cross-applesauce and holding her ankles. "Superwoman." She grinned, then got down to business. "Okay, so, speaking of how you are an unstoppable force of nature and woman, let's get the deets on the contest."

A laugh burst out of Clare. "Laying it on a bit thick, dontcha think?" She was still shaking her head and smiling as she sat on the bed next to Bellamy and pulled out her phone. "All right, it can't hurt to look. Let's see what we're working with."

It didn't take long to pull up the contest details. Clare scrolled slowly down the screen, past photos of loaves of bread and colorful cakes, sugar cookies with intricate detailing, and to the fine print. "Okay, so here's the kicker." She pointed to the entry items. "Each baker needs to present one of each: a cake, a bread, and a cookie. Only one business owner, including cottage kitchens, per team."

"Okay, so that's fine. I'm not a business owner, I'm just a helper. It said you can have one kitchen helper in the contest kitchen."

Clare tapped her lips for a moment, "Yeah, I mean, I guess that does even the field a bit. I wonder if that's why they made that rule."

"To have helpers? I mean, probably because you gotta make enough plates for eight judges, it says. That's a lot of work in a short time span. Even I know that."

"No, no, the rule about not combining companies. The contest says it's for the 'best all around,' but most of us have areas of specialty. Like, some people are really good cookiers and their cookies are colorful and cute and adorable perfection. Some specialize in cakes, like for weddings or birthdays, those elaborate layered cakes. And some specialize more in doughs, like me. We all have our strengths and weaknesses, but basically nobody is perfect at all three."

"But they do all kinds of different things on those baking shows."

"True." Clare clicked on the application button. "But how many of those bakers on those shows will get the top spot one week, and then be in the bottom the next week on a different type of bake?"

"True." Bellamy bit the inside of her lip, then nodded decisively. "So, we'll study. And practice."

Clare turned to her for a minute and then shrugged. "It isn't something we can perfect in the three weeks we have...but what the heck. It's only fifty dollars plus supplies to enter, so mostly all it will do is take time." She gave Bellamy the same stern look she'd given her the many times she'd caught her doodling on the edge of the paper instead of actually completing her math homework. "But it will be time taken during my busiest season. So, if we're going to do this, I need you to be all in. Can you?"

"Yes. I do solemnly swear that I will be here, at your beck and call, until at least the week before Christmas."

Three hours and a table full of stuffed bellies later, Clare stood at the head of the freshly cleared table, holding up a bottle of sparkling wine.

"Tradition!" Adrien hooted from his seat.

"Tradition!" Bellamy cupped a hand to her mouth and called.

"Tradition!" Aunt Gemma and Uncle Richard, their mom's brother and his wife from Graybird, lightly drumrolled on the table.

"Tradition!" Luke pumped a fist in the air.

"Tradition! Tradition! Tradition!" Kevin chanted as he carried the pecan pie over from the counter and set it in front of his wife.

"Traditionally," Clare started with a flourish, "Mom would be here, slicing the pie and popping the bottle." Clare looked around the table at the grinning faces and began twisting the metal wire holding the cork in place. "But this year, we seem to be light on several of our older family members." She set aside the wire cork basket and grabbed the kitchen towel from the back of her chair. "It seems retirement and travel suits them well." She covered the cork with the towel and began to twist. "As such, despite how much we miss them here, we celebrate their joy with our own." The cork exited the bottle with a pop.

Everybody cheered. Even Olivia was given her own glass of sparkling cider. The post-dinner, pre-dessert drink was a Wilson family tradition, with sparkling cider available for anybody who might choose not to drink, but still wanted to participate.

Glasses clinked, and pie was served with big dollops of homemade whipped cream. Bellamy popped the last bite from her own pie into her mouth and looked around, her heart so full it could burst. She couldn't remember a Thanksgiving with so much laughter and banter and genuine love ever happening in LA It had always been quiet, small gatherings of healthy foods with fellow scraping-by models, or mixers and meet and greets and trying to get a leg up in a world of who's who.

"How many more minutes until the dance party?" Olivia looked up from the phone she'd been less than sneaky about texting with off and on throughout the meal under the table.

"Once everybody's finished and the dishes are done," Clare answered, wiping her mouth with her napkin.

"I'll start the dishes," Bellamy offered.

"I'll help!" Olivie popped out of her chair and began circling the table grabbing each empty dessert plate.

Clare's kitchen was separated from the dining table by a bar-style countertop, with a peek-a-boo alcove between the countertop and the cupboard above it.

Bellamy tossed back her remaining sip of champagne as she walked to the oversized divided sink. Once there she settled the delicate flute on the counter behind the faucet and plugged the left side with the rubber stopper, drizzling in dish soap and intermittently swinging the faucet over the right side to rinse and stack plates as they were brought over.

Beside her, the dishwasher chugged and gurgled, washing the bulk of the dishes from the main course.

"Need some help drying?" Luke ambled over, a clean dishtowel thrown over his shoulder.

"That'c be great! I'm embarrassed to admit I don't know where half these dishes go here."

"I like to stash 'em wherever and let Kev guess," Luke said with a wink.

"I guess that could be one way to be uninvited from helping with the dishes in the future." Bellamy chuckled but couldn't help but notice that Luke seemed to know exactly where each item went, eas-ily keeping up with her as she suds and rinsed.

"So, how's LA been treating you?" His hand was gentle as he took the first of the wine glasses from her.

Bellamy squirmed, not wanting to lie, but hating to out herself as a failure. "It's, you know, hot." She answered lamely.

Luke nodded as if it was an interesting answer. "I've heard it cools down pretty good at night this time of year."

"Yep." She popped her lips on the final 'p' sound, not sure how to transition from there. "So, your mom and dad are at Gia and Lucy's for the holidays? When do they get back in town?"

"They're there through the start of the year." Luke turned back from reaching to place the champagne flute on an upper shelf with a grin. "Gia's pregnant."

"What? That's so exciting!" Bellamy shook her head in wonder. Luke's little sister Gia was one grade above in her school and had always been kind.

"Yeah, Mom's over the moon, and you know how much Dad loves babies. I'm planning to head out there just before Christmas, since the baby's due around New Year's."

"You'll have to give her a hug for me. Still in Colorado?"

Luke nodded. "Something about those mountains, Lucy just loves it there."

"Sometimes a place just feels like home." Bellamy looked down as she unplugged the sink drain, not wanting the envy she felt to show on her face.

Olivia flitted over and grabbed the sponge to wipe down the table. "Perfect! Uncle Luke, can you help me and Dad move the table for the dance party? Uncle Adrien's setting up the—"

Before she could finish her sentence the first dancing notes of Mariah Carey's *All I Want for Christmas Is You* chimed out of the speaker blue-toothed to Adrien's phone.

"It's on!" Olivia tossed the sponge back into the sink and did a two-step slide and grapevine out of the kitchen.

"Shall we?" Luke held out his hand.

Bellamy placed her water-wrinkled fingers in his hand without a second thought, the moment too perfect to worry about the little things. He spun them out into the living room area just as the song picked up. The Twinkle lights threaded through the maple leaf garland along the mantle were danc-ing along. Pop song after pop song of Christmas music played as they took turns showing off their best and goofiest dance moves.

Bellamy didn't even notice the cold floor through her thin socks. The scent of pecan pie still hung in the air as they slipped and slid across the wood floor. Laugher floated through the house as adults and Olivia alike twisted and twirled, discoed, and moonwalked.

Eventually, the music was turned down as Un-cle Richard announced that it was time for them to hit the road home. Rounds of hugs happened before everybody pulled on their boots and coats to walk them out to their old Ford.

"It was so good to see you, Honey," Aunt Gem-ma squeezed Bellamy goodbye for the third time before climbing into the passenger seat.

"Drive safe!" Clare called as Uncle Richard started the truck.

The group stood in the chill air, breath puffing, as they waved goodbye.

"I should take a page from their book and call it a night, too." Luke pulled his keys from the pocket of his tan Carhart as everybody else climbed the steps back up to the house.

A chorus of "see you soons" and "goodnights" echoed through the night as everybody shuffled back inside.

Bellamy trailed her siblings in and as she turned to lock the door she saw Luke had left his leftovers and cell phone on the walnut entryway table. "Oh sugar," she muttered, sliding back into her shoes. "I'll be right back," Bellamy called over her shoulder, dashing back out into the cold night.

Luke was getting out of his truck just as she reached the porch, and she met him at the bottom of the stairs, "Hey."

"Hey," he answered, "I forgot my cell."

"Oh, I have it. And your leftovers." She held out the bag of containers in one hand and his phone in the other.

"Thanks, Bells." Luke's hand brushed hers as he took the bag.

Bellamy's fingers tingled at his touch, and his eyes flashed up to meet hers fast enough that she couldn't help but wonder if he felt the same electricity she did. At that moment, a single sparkling snowflake landed on the tip of her nose, drawing her gaze.

"Snow." She grinned and looked around as more clumped flakes floated down around them. She spun in a circle, tipping her back and laughing. "I forgot how beautiful it can be."

Luke smiled slowly, watching her before looking up at the sky himself. "Yeah." He looked back down and met her grin with his own. "Yeah, really beautiful out here tonight."

In his hand, his phone vibrated, and he flicked the screen open as Bellamy tried to catch a snowflake on her tongue. Tucking his phone back in his pocket, he opened his truck door and settled the food bag onto the floor of the passenger seat before turning back to Bellamy. "You should probably get inside before you get too cold."

Bellamy spun again and then grinned up at him. "I know. It's late and I know Clare has a pajama party planned."

Luke paused and then said, "So, you know, if you're really into this 'I missed winter' vibe, I have it on good authority that the pond is getting the final smooth coat this weekend. I'd be happy to take you skating Saturday if the weather holds."

Bellamy bit her lip to stop from beaming too broadly, her heart twinkling like the lights over the mantel. "Yeah... yeah I'd like that a lot."

Chapter Seven

Inside the house, Bellamy floated into the living room where the blow-up mattress was being inflated by two grown men in matching gingerbread-decorated pajamas. The sound of popcorn popping and the aroma of melting butter floated through the peekaboo cutout of Clare's kitchen.

"Your PJs are on your bed," Clare called from the stove.

Humming happily to herself, Bellamy closed the door to the office and finally allowed herself a small squeal of delight. Ice skating might not be a date...but it also just might be one. Maybe. As promised, a pair of brand-new gingerbread-themed pajamas waited for her on the futon. At the top of the pile was a pair of thick, fluffy socks. Dutifully,

Bellamy unbraided her hair and changed into the pajamas before joining her family in the living room.

"How did you know to get these for me?" Bellamy scooted onto the air mattress next to Olivia, who was scrolling through social media while she waited.

"Ah," Clare wrinkled her nose sheepishly as she passed a big green bowl of popcorn to Bellamy before settling onto the couch end right behind Bellamy's head, "Those were actually supposed to be Jonathon's."

It was only then that Bellamy realized her dark green pajamas matched Adrien and Kevin, with Olivia and Clare's gingerbread-themed set having a red background. "Oh." She shrugged. "Too tall for Mom's?"

"Yup." Clare flicked the TV on. "Olivia, phone."

"Mom, I just want to like these posts because other people will like mine and it's just, like, what you do."

"Olivia. You know the rules. I turned a blind eye when you had it at dinner since I know it's hard being the only teenager in a group of adults. But, now, it's movie and popcorn and family bonding, and if we all don't have our phones, you don't need yours."

The tradition of the family having a big sleepover in matching pajamas had started the first year after the divorce. The old holiday traditions felt sad and empty, like a reminder that somebody was missing. Bellamy had only been eight. So, their mother had started new traditions. Back then, they'd turned the ringer off on the house phone during the movie marathon of the old Rudolph the Red Nose Reindeer. They'd pile pillows and blankets on the floor in front of the couch and all spend the night of Thanksgiving in front of the TV, transitioning from fall to Christmas.

Now that landlines were a thing of the past, the rule was that all cell phones were silent and piled on the table.

After a long moment of tension, Olivia shrugged. "Fine," she said, stomping over to add her phone to the pile.

Once everyone was settled in their preferred spaces—Adrien in the leather recliner, Clare and Kevin on the couch, and Olivia and Bellamy with the pile of pillows and blankets on the air mattress in front of the couch, Clare pressed the play button.

Despite her afternoon nap, it didn't take long for Olivia to fall asleep. After Rudolph saved the day, Bellamy slipped the popcorn bowl away from Olivia's arm and turned to get Clare's attention...only to find that both Clare and Kevin had fallen asleep as well.

"Does this always happen?" She whispered to Adrien as she gingerly lifted the half-full popcorn bucket from between her sister and brother-in-law.

He held a finger to his lips, grabbing a blanket and motioning for her to follow him.

She set the popcorn dishes down on the table as she passed and she followed her big brother to the entryway, where he was zipping up his coat and stepping into his boots.

"Hey." He wrapped the blanket around her and motioned for her to slip on her own shoes. "Let's talk."

Bellamy sighed. She'd known he wasn't going to just drop it. Probably the biggest trait they all had in common was stubbornness.

They settled onto the top porch step, watching the snow, no longer falling in big picturesque clumps, but still just as glittery in the moonlight.

"Remember when you used to make me sit out at the picnic table in the backyard in the summers so you could practice your astrology? Because you were too afraid of the dark to sit outside alone." Adrien snickered, shaking his head.

"It was astronomy. It's a science." Bellamy sniffed daintily.

"The only constellations you ever looked for were the zodiac signs...and then you'd read to me from the big book of fortunes."

"Okay, fine, maybe it was both," Bellamy admitted.

Adrien clasped his hands together, his elbows resting on either knee. "You always did like that kind of stuff. Artsy, creative, a dreamer. I guess it wasn't really a surprise you had to try your hand at LA."

"I wasn't just trying my hand at LA. I worked really hard, it wasn't just some whim." He'd always been able to get under her skin.

He picked at a hangnail on his thumb, thinking for a long moment before answering. "Look, Belly B, I'm not trying to argue with you here. I'm just trying to say that, you know, I'm proud of you for being brave. I know it wasn't a whim."

"Oh." She placed her hands down on either side of her hips, grounding herself with the cool wood against the palms of her hands.

"And I know you worked hard. From what Clare tells me, you got a pretty unfair shake from that boss of yours."

"Yeah." Bellamy felt the tears welling up in her eyes. She sincerely did not want to have to explain all over again what a fool she'd been to trust Amma. How she'd seen the terrible way her ex-boss had treated people, how she'd watched her use and abuse person after person. But how she'd been stupid enough to think if she worked hard enough, it wouldn't happen to her.

"How bad is it?" Adrien cleared his throat. "If you need money, I can float you. But just...really take stock of what you want."

"I don't want your money." Bellamy thought about how much easier it would be to take his loan than to hope for some long-shot baking contest. But how would she ever pay him back? What if she failed again?

Adrien nodded and bumped her shoulder with his. "Okay. But, kid, there's no shame in a pivot."

"What would you know? You went from football star to being practically the town mayor without a single moment of doubt." It was hard to swallow advice from the golden child.

"Whoa, whoa, whoa. Real Estate King, thank you. I'm not into politics." He shook his head and then added more quietly, "It really wasn't like that. Listen, Bellamy, I didn't really talk about it at the time because I was scared and angry and honestly should have gone to therapy sooner to deal with it. But, now I have, and now I can say it." He turned to her, his light brown eyes so much like the ones she looked at in the mirror every day.

Bellamy nodded, waiting for him to continue. She hadn't known he'd gone to therapy.

"When I blew out my knee, everything I thought I knew about myself seemed like it'd been blown to pieces. I thought all I was, all I'd ever wanted to be, was being a running back. You know, football was my life. I only went to college at all because Mom and Dad made us. Then, the first thing Dad said when he came to the hospital was that I'd blown my chances at the NFL."

Bellamy shook her head. Their dad had pretty much only been around after the divorce when Adrien had a football game. He'd forget all about her and Clare's birthdays, but he'd never miss a Friday night.

"In that moment, I felt like he'd never bother with me again. And I was basically right."

"He's a jerk."

"Yeah, he is. Sometimes people just are. But, here's the thing. Here's what I learned. That you are more than a single plan. And that we don't need to try to earn love that isn't freely given."

Bellamy swallowed and swiped at the tears streaking down her face. "Who even are you?"

Adrien snorted. "Look, yeah, it's mushy and all self-helpy or whatever. But I guess I just want you to know...even if you never become a movie star, or own a modeling company, or even if you never go back to LA. You're enough, Bellamy." He ran a hand down his face and blew out a huff of air. "But, yeah. Enough of the daytime tv talk show touchy feely stuff."

"How long did it take you to know what to do instead?" The ache that had been sitting like a ball in the pit of her stomach for months now felt numb. It wasn't gone, but it wasn't as painful.

"Longer than it looked like from the outside."

"When did you know what the right job was for you?" She leaned against him, and let her head rest on his shoulder, pulling the blanket tighter around herself. "Like, how did you know you weren't just going to fail if you tried something new?"

Adrien was quiet, and they watched the snow for several minutes before he answered. "I thought of it like a pivot. Sometimes, you have to try a pivot to the left to shake the guy on defense. Other times, it's a big zag to the right. The only thing that never works is to not pivot. If you stand still, you never get the ball."

"Huh." Bellamy digested the words, not sure how exactly they applied to her own life.

"And maybe the first move you make doesn't work. Then you try a different one. Something not working out isn't the end of the play; it's a learning opportunity."

"You know, for a meathead big brother, you were doing pretty good at being sweet and wise."

"Yeah, well." He reached over and tousled her hair. "Just make sure you don't tell anyone. I have a reputation to maintain as a meathead."

Bellamy snorted, then nudged him with her elbow. "Thanks, bro."

Chapter Eight

"Here, look at this one." Clare angled her phone to Bellamy, showing her a set of blue and gold cookies shaped like the letter M and footballs. "This is a cottage baker out of Ypsi."

Bellamy nodded, reaching over to scroll to the next image posted by the baker. "Ohh, I like how they used the shimmery frosting on these fish scales."

Bellamy held up her own phone. "This one is a baker from Lansing and she has the cutest narwhal set. Or look at this winter set she made. The trees have gold sugar that looks like twinkle lights. Smart and pretty."

Beside them, the oven dinged, and Clare bustled over to take the sugar cookies from the shelf on the walk-in fridge over to it. They both winced at the shriek the metal made as it slid against the sides of the oven.

"Maybe you should have replaced all the ovens, that's obnoxious." Bellamy wrinkled her nose and set the timer.

"When we win, maybe I will." Clare made a note of the minutes on the timer and the temp of the oven in her notebook before they went back to scrolling through social media for inspiration.

Nothin' But Sugar was traditionally closed the day after Thanksgiving each year since Clare's philosophy was that most people would have left-over pie and bread to eat still anyhow. So, as promised, she and Bellamy were studying up on their weakest area for the contest: cookies.

"Okay, so I've been looking at cookie accounts for an hour now, and I keep coming back to this one." Bellamy held her phone out to show Clare the cookie set that depicted sushi, a lucky cat, and a kite. Once Clare nodded, she scrolled to show a set with a cartoon kitty in a hula skirt next to a cookie that looked like a girl doing the hula with a plumeria flower in her hair. "Look at the details. And how it's themed for where the baker lives. Like this poké bowl one has so many different textures to the decorations. That's what I want to learn to do."

Clare squinted at the screen and nodded, "Yeah, it really adds something more to it. What's the company name? I want to follow them."

"You Made This For Me, no spaces for the social media handle. From Hawaii, how cool is that?" Bellamy went back to the main search bar and typed in "cookies," scrolling through more colorful cookies of all shapes and sizes. "It's really pretty amazing how beautiful these cookies are. Why'd you focus on bread when you could have done this?"

Clare barked out a laugh, shaking her head. "For many reasons. Mostly because I am not a good decorator. I can't pipe a clean line to save my life if I'm taking my time...let alone if I'm mass producing. Plus, all the shapes and themes make it something you need constant new supplies for. I like the stability of bread. If you do the science right, it never lets you down."

"You decorate your pies nicely—"

"With pie crust that I use the cookie cutters for year after year."

"Okay, fine. But you sometimes try new stuff, like when you added red swirls to the pie crust for the maple leaves. Speaking of pies...have you thought much about the cake aspect?"

The timer dinged, and Clare peeked into the oven, then set it for another minute. "I have. I can't compete with the structured stuff. You know, big layers, carved to look like a specific thing. We don't do that here, and we don't have the equipment or the time to learn both cakes and cookies. So, it's going to have to be a real winner by flavor."

The timer dinged again. Clare slid her hands into the silicone oven mitts, pulling the tray of cookies out and setting it aside to cool.

"Okay." Bellamy nodded. "So, flavor focus for cake, something cool and fancy for bread, and then a really good sugar cookie that I will figure out how to make beyond adorable." She took a deep breath, the warm buttery scent of the cookies beside her calming her nerves. "Yeah, we can do this."

"Good. Now, I want you to research what you need to be able to decorate well. We can do a small supply run later today when the worst of the shopping crowds have gotten their toys and TVs. I'm going to do some cake planning." Clare began shuffling the cookies onto a cooling rack.

Bellamy broke the corner off a pine tree–shaped cookie and placed it in her mouth. "It's a lit-tle...sandy."

Clare frowned and took a taste herself. "Yeah. Okay, so I'll adjust." She scribbled in her note-book, noting how well the cookies held their shape, and some texture and flavor details that Bellamy couldn't read because she wasn't even sure if her sister was writing actual letters or just squiggles.

After a few hours of watching videos online and reading articles, Bellamy had a mental list of things she'd need. Gel food coloring would be key. Mylar food-safe plastic sheets to make stencils with. An airbrush would be really helpful to develop more nuance to the coloring. Luster dust and maybe some little pearls or sprinkles and other decorative candies would help too. Maybe some cookie cutters, if they had ones that would work for their design.

Clare had been in her office flipping through cookbooks, with the occasional sigh or happy hum floating out to Bellamy where she sat on the countertop by the sink.

Bellamy slid off the counter and grabbed Clare's notebook, flipping to some empty pages in the back. She tapped the pen against her lower lip, thinking about what sort of theme they should make their cookies. She made a list of what she knew the contest factored in: the holidays, local bakers only, it would be televised.

Unsure where to start, Bellamy sketched out some basic holiday items. After a candy cane, a stocking, and a gift with a big bow, she moved on to more Michigan-based themes. First, she sketched the Great Lakes, then the Mackinac Bridge. She sketched a car, a Spartan, and a Wolverine. Nothing felt quite right.

By the time Clare walked out of her office, Bellamy had filled pages with wreaths and strings of lights, decorated trees, fish, lakes, mittens, and more.

"I'm not saying 'no,' but I'm really curious how you are going to fit those ideas into a theme for this contest." Clare tapped the page Bellamy was doodling on.

"Oh." Bellamy looked down and felt just as guilty as she had all those years at the kitchen table. Once again, she'd been caught drawing elaborate dresses and little shirt and skirt combos instead of focusing on her assignment. "Sorry, guess my mind wandered." She flipped to the prior pages of sketches. "Do any of these look like they could be winners?"

Clare studied the drawings, tilting her head this way and that, looking at the details on the ones with more decorations. "I think I see a lot of good potential. I guess we need to figure out if we want to have a theme throughout. You know, match the whole plate to one idea."

"I was thinking the same thing!" Bellamy beamed. It was nice to know they were on the same page. It was almost as if she could feel the warmth of the LA sun already.

"Ready to go head out for supplies? It's going to take a lot of practice to decorate with the details you have in mind."

"Yep, ready." Bellamy nodded, feeling a small bead of sweat drip down her back. Confused, she turned and saw that the oven she stood directly in front of was still on. "I think leaving with the oven on is a safety hazard."

Clare rolled her eyes to the ceiling and heaved a big sigh. "It absolutely is. We're going to bed early tonight," she said as she flipped the oven off. "Tomorrow the bakery is back to normal hours."

"What time does that mean we have to be in?"

"You can sleep in if you want. Maybe work on some sketches. I know I said you'd be helping here, but you can have a day off. Olivia can hang out at the counter for a few hours while I get the initial baking done."

"You sure?"

"Absolutely. Besides, I heard The Pond was smoothed over today, so maybe you and Olivia can go skate before you drop her off at the theater for rehearsal."

Bellamy felt her cheeks heat. She hadn't told anyone about her maybe-date yet. "Actually, I *was* kind of hoping to go ice skating tomorrow. Luke invited me. But," she added quickly, "of course Olivia can come too. And I can definitely take her to rehearsal. I can borrow the van, right?"

Clare smirked, "Oh really? Skating with Luke? Do you remember the last time you went skating with a group that included Luke?"

"That's not going to happen again." Bellamy gave her sister a narrow-eyed glare.

"Mmmhmm. It better not. Anyhow, that's fine, Olivia can hang here and work on her biology paper until you take her to rehearsal. Yes, with the van."

"Thanks, Clare, Clare the Mother Bear."

"Alright, alright already, let's go get some supplies." Clare shooed Bellamy toward the back door of the bakery.

Chapter Nine

Bellamy was deeply engrossed in practicing an ombre effect with the airbrush on a piece of paper towel when the doorbell rang. "Eep!" She glanced at the clock and quickly shoved her bangs off her forehead, swiping her fingers above each eye to smooth her brows before answering the door.

"Hey Bells, ready to go ska—that's a really interesting makeup choice. Sort of, uh, creative." Luke's green eyes were dancing as he tried to find the right words.

"Thanks," Bellamy answered absently, silently cursing herself for getting caught up in her cookie project and losing track of time. She'd wanted to change and do her makeup before Luke came to pick her up. "Wait...what? I'm not wearing any makeup."

Luke's eyebrows jumped up and he was now pressing his lips together, but Bellamy could still see the laughter he was trying to hide.

"What?" She dashed to the bathroom, horror spreading through her as she put the pieces together. "No. No, no, no, no. Ugh." The green food coloring she'd been using with the airbrush must have gotten on her hands. "I'll be, uh, I'll be out soon!" She called through the bathroom door, turning the tap on. Staring at herself in the mirror, Bellamy didn't know if she wanted to laugh or cry. Of course her first maybe date with the guy she'd had a huge crush on in high school was going to be marred by the fact that she had a green streak across her forehead...and two bright green smudges outlining her eyebrows.

"Argh!" Bellamy grabbed a round cotton pad from the stack beside her makeup remover and doused it with the oily liquid. Frantically, she scrubbed at the green streaks. Very little happened. "Oh come on, come on." She rubbed harder, but only ended up looking like she was starting a transformation into The Grinch with her now green eyebrow hairs sticking up.

A light knock sounded on the door. "Everything okay in there?"

"I..." She pumped some hand soap from the dispenser and worked it into her eyebrows, rubbing it vigorously into the green streak on her forehead.

"Bells?"

She rinsed her face in the sink, and when she finished patting the water off, was pleased to see the green had faded. A little. But it was still there. She could try to cover it with foundation. Maybe some highlighting contouring cream first. But the bulk of her makeup was in the office. Which meant she'd have to face Luke again.

"Look, Bellamy, I'm sorry I laughed. It's really not a big deal. Want me to streak my face too?"

Giving herself one last look in the mirror, Bellamy shrugged and opened the bathroom door. "I do have the airbrush ready still if you're serious."

"Could you make it a good design?" Luke was leaning against the wall beside the bathroom door, looking totally relaxed.

"Not yet, but I can do a pretty good ombre. Want it to go dark to light from the forehead down?" She gestured over the table where she'd been practicing.

Luke walked over to the table and picked up a bottle of the liquid food dye, looking at the ingredients. "What'd you use in there to try to get it off?"

"Makeup remover and then when that didn't work, soap." Bellamy looked at her hands, where her fingers were still green as well.

Luke nodded. "Right. Well, on the plus side, you'll be wearing a hat, so it won't be as noticeable. You ready?"

"What? No. I mean, I can't go like this." She gestured to her face. It was one thing to be seen with a messy ponytail and her old high school hoodie being helpful at the bakery, and another thing entirely to look like maybe she was actually back from LA due to her face starting to mold.

"I really don't think anyone in Treeview is going to care."

"But I care." Bellamy huffed. Then she remembered she was in her sweatpants still. "Okay. You're right, I have to be back at the bakery by four to take Olivia to rehearsal. I'll just wear my hat really low. Give me five minutes to change." Bellamy had tried on three different combinations of jeans and long-sleeved thermal shirts that morning. She had the perfect outfit picked out, thanks to Olivia loaning her a puffy vest and a cute mitten and hat set.

"You really don't need to change..." Luke trailed off as Bellamy disappeared into her makeshift bedroom.

When Bellamy came back out less than five minutes later, Luke had his phone in one hand and the boxed package the food dye bottle set had come in in the other.

"Sorry about that, I'm ready now." Bellamy had the knitted red winter hat pulled as low as she could get it to stay.

"I was just looking at the website for the manufacturer, and it suggests using hand sanitizer on skin stains." Luke set the box back down and grabbed a paper towel, pumping two squirts from the bottle of hand sanitizer Clare always kept on the end of the counter.

He stepped closer to Bellamy and gently pushed the hat up. "Let's just give this a try."

Bellamy was frozen, breathing in the minty scent of whatever shaving cream he'd used. "Okay," she squeaked out. When Luke tipped her chin up with the brush of his thumb, a glow of warmth spread, causing her breath to hitch.

"Just a few quick moments." He smoothed the wet paper towel across her forehead. "Go ahead and close your eyes for me, Bells."

She swallowed hard. His face was mere inches from hers, his voice soft and silky smooth. She did as he asked.

The alcohol felt cool as he traced her eyebrows, slow and steady.

"Okay, go take a look." The moment was broken when Luke stepped away.

Suddenly chilly without the warmth radiating from him, Bellamy briskly rubbed her arms and went to look in the mirror.

"Holy cannoli, it worked!" Her eyebrows were a mostly normal color now. The streak on her forehead was faintly visible but would be easily covered by the winter hat. "You're amazing." She beamed at him.

"Easy day. Ready?" Luke gestured toward the door.

The route to The Pond was straight through Mainstreet. As they passed Nothin' But Sugar, Bellamy saw a woman leaving with a basket of goodies. Business seemed to be really steady. Bellamy fought down her jealousy. It was silly to be envious of her sister instead of proud of her...yet she still couldn't help comparing herself.

"Been a while since you were here last. Did anybody show you the changes?" Luke reached over and turned the radio down.

"Does anything ever really change much here?" Bellamy asked as they passed the same floral shop that had been on the corner for decades.

Luke glanced over at her before answering, "Sometimes I think that's the beauty of it here. You'll always have these nice pockets of community-owned businesses instead of corporate warehouses. There are a million concrete jungles...but me, I like this. A forest with hiking less than a ten-minute drive away. The bay on one of the world's largest freshwater lakes only fifteen minutes walk from downtown. I wouldn't have it any other way."

Bellamy studied him as he spoke, the easy affection in his voice warm and inviting. "You really don't ever want to leave Treeview?"

"Nah. This is it for me. Where else can I get paid to climb trees?" He shot her the boyish grin that she'd first fallen for.

"I think you get paid to trim them, not to climb them." She couldn't help but smile back at him. "But you do make it sound awfully appealing here." When Luke turned left toward the old repurposed tennis court Bellamy stared at the colorful playground that appeared.

"Told you there were some new things." Luke slowed the truck further so Bellamy could take in the bright jungle gym, mini climbing wall, and the two slides connected by a plank bridge.

"Wow. Yeah, I guess so. When did this go in?"

"'Bout a year and a half ago. Last summer they were out here in the July heat wave putting it all together. The Business Association raised the funds." He pointed to the big square next to the curly slide. "They even had the school speech therapy team consult on this communication board thing. Makes it more accessible." He pointed to a wall shaped like a ribbon, with many curves. "And that wall thing has different alcoves in it for sensory things. Like a quiet spot with acoustic absorption, a spinning seat, that sort of thing."

"In Treeview?" Bellamy had no idea their town even thought about such things. All they'd had growing up was a metal stand with some hot black swings attached to chains. The kind that always burnt the back of her legs on a hot summer day.

"Yeah, in Treeview." Luke returned to the speed limit, cruising past the two-screen movie theater. In moments, they were pulling into the parking area for The Pond. There had once been a small, members-only country club in Treeview, back in the forties. When it closed, the township purchased the land and repurposed it. They'd restored two of the tennis courts and used the other for The Pond. A small retaining wall had been built around it, and each year the court was flooded with water.

"Here we go." Luke put the truck in park. "They still do the rentals out of the old guard shack, just like before." He opened his door. "Because you're right, most things don't change."

Bellamy hopped down from the truck and walked around to Luke's side as he was getting something out of the back seat. "Don't tell me you still have your old hockey skates," she teased.

Luke chuckled, "Oh no...I get a new pair every few years. They're getting sharpened for the season right now. What I have here," he said, turning, "is for you." And he gently settled a helmet over her hat.

"What? Hey! I'm not wearing this thing. Where'd you even get it."

"Do you remember the last time we went skating together?" He stepped closer to clip the chin strap.

"Why does everyone keep bringing that up?"

"It was traumatic," he said with a carefully straight face.

"For whom?" Bellamy glared up at him. "Besides, I'm not twelve anymore. It's been years."

The corner of his mouth inched up. "And how many times have you been skating since then?"

"Plenty. I skated a lot in high school."

"And how long ago was high school?" He was positively smirking. "Besides, it was traumatizing. Darlene Bander never said a single nice word to me again."

"What a terrible shame for you." She stomped off toward the guard shack to get a pair of skates, calling over her shoulder, "Besides, I broke my arm, not my head!'

"Did you want wrist braces instead, then?" Luke easily matched her pace.

"No. I'm taking this off." She stopped and faced him, giving him her most stern face. "It doesn't go with my outfit at all. Besides, you're not wearing one." She unclipped the chin strap.

"I skate every winter. And I've never broken a bone." He reached out and reclipped the helmet buckle, leaning closer to say quietly, "Besides, you look cute in my climbing gear."

Butterflies danced low in her belly as she took in the minty scent of him again. "How do you smell so good?" She mumbled.

A slow smile spread across his lips. "I didn't realize I did."

Bellamy traced the line of his lips with her eyes, wondering what it would feel like to lean those few inches further in and press her own mouth to his.

"Next!" The teen at the counter called loudly, ringing a bell in their direction and breaking the spell.

Luke turned and held up two fingers, "Two pairs, please. Size eleven and..."

"I'll take a women's 8, please." Bellamy stepped over the counter, willing her heart rate to normalize.

To Bellamy's relief, there weren't many skaters out. With the weather often above freezing, it could be hit or miss between Thanksgiving and Christmas. It didn't take long for them to change out of their shoes and into the skates.

Luke held out a hand to her, "Clare did clearly state that if you broke your arm this time she would hold me personally responsible."

Bellamy placed her mittened hand in his, glad that they had the buffer of cloth to stop all the distracting feelings. Despite her earlier bravado, it had been many years since she'd last skated, and tromping over the rubber mats around The Pond was no easy task.

"It was Adrien's fault I fell anyhow." Bellamy had been a fifth-wheel tag-along on Adrien's date the night of the incident. "He was showing off for Liz, you remember?"

Luke smoothly skated backward on the ice, holding out his other hand for her to stabilize with as she transitioned from clomping across rubber to wobbling on ice. "I do."

As if on cue, the speakers rigged around The Pond switched from country music to a crooning rendition of *I'll Be Home for Christmas.*

"Did Darlene really never talk to you again?" She pushed forward with one skate, gaining more confidence.

Luke let go of her right hand, swinging around to skate beside her now. "I said she never said a *nice* word to me again. She had a few choice words for me the next time Adrien suggested a double date."

Bellamy snorted. "Well, now I feel a little bad. I had no idea." When she'd fallen, Adrien had been unable to reach their mother right away. He didn't want to end his date, so Luke had volunteered to walk her the three blocks over to the hospital and stay with her while they called her mom again.

"Oh, don't feel bad. Goofing off and trying to keep your mind off how scared you were was a lot more fun than trying to avoid sweaty Darlene's hands."

"Oh really? Then why'd you even go on the date?" That night had been the moment her crush on Luke had materialized. He'd gone from her brother's teasing friend to the cutest, nicest, handsomest guy she'd ever known. At least for the next few years. Her crush had faded when she'd started dating guys her own age. Until now, when their four-year age gap felt normal, and there was definitely something sizzling in the air between them every time he got close.

"Your brother. Liz's parents were strict, and she wasn't technically allowed to date. Which is why myself, Darlene, and even you, were there."

"Oh. And all this time I thought he took me because I wanted to go. Adrien!" She mockingly shook her fist at the sky and promptly lost her balance.

Luke pulled her in and used his free hand to steady her. "Maybe we'll skate this way for a while," he offered, giving her his right hand again, skating backward.

"Thanks." Bellamy got back into the rhythm, gliding smoothly again. "You are an obnoxiously good skater." She smiled to soften her words.

"I haven't even gotten to the part where I show off." He squeezed her hand.

There was something vulnerable in his eyes when Bellamy looked up, a tenderness she hadn't seen before.

"Unless of course, you just want to do a few easy laps and enjoy the moment." He offered, his tone even and unrevealing. "In which case," he added in a lighter tone, "I can completely avoid the pressure of showing off."

"This is actually pretty perfect," she replied because it really was.

Chapter Ten

When Luke dropped her off at Nothin' But Sugar, Bellamy still didn't know if the ice skating was a date or not. Probably not. It hadn't ended in a kiss. But there had been moments when she was sure she wasn't the only one feeling the electricity between them.

"Oh good, you made it! I was starting to worry." Clare popped out of the kitchen when the bell above the door announced Bellamy's entrance. "Olivia is finishing her paper in my office, but last I checked she was in the proofreading stage. How was skating?" Clare paused in her bustle and studied Bellamy's flushed cheeks and giddy grin. "Looks like it was fun."

"It was perfect. I mean." Bellamy felt her cheeks heat and tried to hide how flustered she suddenly felt. It was one thing to fawn over Luke as a teen, and entirely different at almost thirty. "I mean it was perfect weather and The Pond was pretty empty, so I didn't have to dodge many little kids, which helped."

"Aunty Baa Baa! I'm ready." Olivia trotted through the swinging door, a backpack slung over her shoulder and Clare's keys in her hands.

"Let's hit the road, then." Bellamy snagged the keys, and with a wave to Clare, they both headed toward the back door.

"Love you, Mom!" Olivia called just before the heavy metal back door closed.

Once they were buckled in, Bellamy inched the van back, glad that the roads were clear and there hadn't been any fresh snow.

"How long does rehearsal usually last?" Bellamy drove past the grocery store and the florist, then nodded as Olivia pointed to the right, putting on her turn signal.

"Mm, well sometimes it's pretty short and sometimes it's kind of longer. It depends on what part of the show they're working on. Mr. Anvack, he's the director, doesn't like to make the full cast stay unless they're running the scenes with us in it. So, today I'm going in early to help Miss Everly with the costumes. Melly can't come because they're at her grandparent's house for the holiday weekend."

Bellamy pulled into the remodeled building. What used to be an empty corrugated metal rectangle that had once been used seasonally for haunted houses and a variety of campaign headquarters was now a beautiful golden wood cabin-fronted theater. Bellamy looked at the sign, painted to look like the letters were spelled in pine tree branches: The Pine. Creativity was maybe not the township council's strong suit when it came to naming things.

"This looks so good," Bellamy gushed, putting the van in park.

"I know." Olivia was grinning ear to ear. "I bet if it was here when you were my age you would have starred in every production."

Bellamy raised her eyebrows. "I bet if it was here when I was your age, I too would have played ensemble parts unless the show had a teenage main character. And even then, who knows." She wondered if she would have moved to LA if she hadn't gotten the leads in all of her school plays. Maybe she'd been too much of a big fish in a small pond. She'd certainly expected to get a lot more roles a lot faster in LA.

"Whatever, I think you're just being modest. Mom has all the scenes you were in recorded on the DVR at home. The ones from that wizard movie series, and the three different TV shows. Plus, Grandma has all the newspaper reviews from when you were in high school. She keeps them in the same book as Uncle Adrien's football articles. So...I know you're a star."

Bellamy stepped out of the van, shaking her head. She wouldn't disillusion her niece. It was actually nice to have the reminder that even though she'd never gotten a big break, she had done some cool things in LA. It meant something to be a regular extra on a show, even if you never had a speaking part. It was a reminder that there could be more to come when she went back with different priorities.

"Thanks, Livvy. That's real sweet. Now, you lead the way, because this is your production, and you are the star here, not me."

Olivia beamed and hitched her backpack on her shoulder, skipping easily up the sidewalk to the big glass doors. "Okay, so first there's the lobby." She gestured around, her voice bounding off the polished wood floors and high ceilings. "The auditorium is probably locked for another hour or two. Here's the bathrooms." Olivia walked confidently past the rows of double doors and then gestured to the small hallway next to the auditorium doors. "And down here," she said, pulling open a door, "is the hall to the backstage area."

Bellamy followed her. There was something magical about getting to be in the hushed, and often frantic, backstage areas of a live performance. Even in this newer theater, it was as if the walls had absorbed the excitement, nerves, and energy of the performers. She used to imagine that if she listened hard enough in the few quiet moments, she could hear the faint echo of actors and actresses of the past practicing their lines.

Olivia held up a finger to her mouth and motioned for Bellamy to follow her through a door painted black. It was dark, and Olivia pulled back a heavy curtain to reveal a single light, sitting on a rolling stand, glowing in the middle of the empty stage.

"Ghostie" Olivia whispered.

At the same time, Bellam whispered, "The ghost light."

The light was traditionally left on in theaters, superstitiously to either ward off spirits or keep a friendly theater ghost company. Realistically, it was so that the first person on the stage to open the theater could find a light switch without falling off the edge of the stage.

"Jinx! Sort of." Olivia giggled and let the curtain fall closed, backing them out of the door and continuing down the hall. "That's the guy's dressing area." She gestured to a navy blue door on the right. "And here is the girl's." She ran a hand along the crimson door on the left as they passed it. "And here," she announced, flourishing grandly at a deep purple door, "is the costuming department." She knocked on the door before turning the handle and opening it.

The room was an explosion of fabrics and wheeled wardrobe racks. Three sewing machines sat on two long white folding tables. Sitting amongst the chaos was a tiny woman with wild gray curls floating around her head, and about four pins gripped in the corner of her mouth.

She looked up from the cloth she was studying through the thick purple glasses perched on the end of her nose and did a little wiggle of her fingers before popping a pin out of her mouth and sliding it into the layers of fabric.

"Olivia! Darling, so happy you made it! Who is this new helper?" She spoke as if she didn't have tiny pointy objects tottering between her lips.

"Miss Everly, this is my aunt Bellamy. She's just here to drop me off."

Bellamy took in the stacks of folded cloth with drawings and noted measurements beside the sewing machines. "Hi, nice to meet you. Are, um, well. I mean, I can help if you need it. When do dress rehearsals start?"

"Two weeks. Oh yes, it's a tall bill. Olivia has been such a helper. Melanie, too." Miss Everly shoved another pin into the next chalk mark. "Do you sew?"

"I can do the basics," Bellamy answered. It was true that she'd done some altering and tailoring of her own clothes, or her other paycheck-paycheck friend's clothes. She'd also done a lot of last-minute fixes for models on photo sets, but those were usually more of a trick of the eye and careful pinning or taping.

"Oh, good, good. Olivia has really shown a knack for it. And she is an ace at threading the machines." Miss Everly stuck a final pin in, and then set aside the rough cloth in her lap. "So, here is the list of what we've to do, and here is what's been pinned and measured and is ready for stitching."

"Oh my gosh, this is so cool! You're really going to stay and help?" Olivia slung her backpack into a corner and moved over to the sewing machine tables, pulling up a small stool.

"Yeah. Yeah, I'm happy to." Bellamy ignored the fact that she had intended to spend the evening looking at roommate ads for LA apartments in the hopes of finding one that didn't seem like a secret murderer.

Miss Everly clapped her hands together twice. "Wonderful! Wonderful!"

Three hours later, Bellamy stretched, rotating her head from side to side, and groaned when her neck cracked.

"Not bad, darling, not bad at all." Miss Everly shook out the dress Bellamy had sewn lace edging onto the shoulders, wrist cuffs, and hem of. "It's almost a shame we'll have to distress it a bit since it is for the Cratchit family."

"Thanks. Yeah, it's not as fun to muck up something you've just worked so hard on." Bellamy stretched and curled her fingers, studying the pile of cream-colored bonnets sitting in a stack between her and the sewing machine Olivia had been at before being called up for a run-through of the final scene at the Cratchit house.

Miss Everly checked her watch. "Rehearsal's just about finished, darlingest. Why don't you run on up and see if you can catch Joy, the stage manager, and make sure she gets your name for the costuming department for the program."

"Oh, no, that's so kind of you, but it's not necessary."

"It absolutely is. One of the things I have been teaching these young ones is that every person who works on a production is a key piece of it. From the ushers to the star actors. Each hand that helps, matters." She shook a gnarled finger in Bellamy's direction. "Don't you go undoing my hard work." She hung the dress on the wardrobe rack, taping a label to the hanger. "Plus, I'm hoping, rather selfishly, that maybe we can snag you to help a bit more next week. Olivia and Melanie, those darlings, will be lost to me when tech rehearsals start, and I fear I've spent more time teaching than I ought to have."

"Oh, ah." Bellamy hedged, knowing that she had already promised Clare to help at the bakery, and she'd told Adrien she'd help decorate their mom's house so that when they came home on Christmas Eve it would be festive and fun. Not to mention that she needed to be applying for at least some temp jobs in LA and figuring out her living situation. Oh, and of course trying to learn enough cookie decorating skills to hold her own for the contest so that she could actually go back to LA as planned.

Miss Everly waved a hand in the air as if to clear out a bad smell. "Don't worry about it. I didn't mean to overstep." She sighed heavily. "We will get it sorted, one way or another."

Bellamy winced internally, but said, "I think I can help at least one more night for a few hours. I'll offer to bring Olivia later this week, and I'll stay again.

Please feel free to plan out what you need me to do and I'll get as much done as I can."

"You, my darling, are an angel. A Christmas miracle, one might say." She tapped the side of her nose, nodding.

Chapter Eleven

"I have an idea for a theme." Bellamy sipped her coffee, still not sure if she was fully awake.

Clare looked over from where she was kneading dough. "Hm?"

"For the cookies." Another drink of coffee, this time a large gulp. "I mean, the whole plate."

"Okay. Could you maybe do some measuring while you're explaining?" Clare gestured to the sacks of flour, baking powder, and sugar beside Bellamy. "And use the scale, for the sake of my headache."

Bellamy chugged the rest of her coffee and rolled up the sleeves of her sparkling red sweater. "I know, I know. It's not my fault you didn't tell me to use the kitchen scale for the donuts when you dragged me here at three in the morning." She looked at the rack of beautifully fried donuts, a treat only served at Nothin' But Sugar on Sunday mornings. "Besides, they turned out great."

"Luckily, donuts are more forgiving than this pie crust you're measuring for next." Clare punched the dough she was working with down, then began folding it together again. "Anyhow, what's your idea?"

Bellamy washed her hands thoroughly, taking her time to really let the idea simmering in her brain solidify. "So, it's still rough, but you know how the contest is local?"

"Mmhmm."

"And it's holiday themed."

"Yep." Another thumping for the bread punctuated Clare's response.

"So, basically we are all going to be thinking the same themes. Probably everybody will do decorated trees and stockings and Santa and that kind of thing. Maybe some Menorahs or oil lamps, something like that."

Clare sliced the dough into five equal pieces, slathered it with rosemary-infused oil, and settled each piece gently into individual bread pans. "Right, yeah, so what's your plan?" She eyed Bellamy's work sifting flour into the plastic bin on the scale.

"So probably we don't want to do those things."

"You want to avoid any holiday themed decorations for a holiday baking contest?" Clare's skepticism was obvious even with her back turned as she thrust the bread pans into the oven.

"Yes. I mean, no, we will definitely still have to make it holiday-themed. But..." She trailed off, the idea she'd come up with on the drive into the bakery feeling like an epic failure now that she was voicing it out loud.

"Belly Baby, just spit it out." Clare swiped her hands on her apron and bustled over to her open recipe book.

"Right, yeah. I was thinking what if we did a 'Tree-view Through the Ages' sort of theme." She paused to check the number on the scale and compare it to the weight on the list for flour. Adding one more half cup to the sifter, she continued, "So, we'd have maybe a decoration on the cake top that looks like the town sign. And then we could have some cookies that look like the more historic buildings, and we could add some cookies for the newer initiatives."

"You want to make cookies shaped like real buildings?" Clare was now whisking powdered sugar and something orange in a metal bowl. "And you want us to decorate the cake, which is supposed to be a flavor star with a clean and simple design?"

"You hate it."

"No." Clare stared into the bowl as she whisked, brows furrowed. "I actually kind of like the idea. We'd have to be precise. The buildings or features would need to be recognizable. But...it could be like a love letter to the community."

"Right! Exactly. Because some people," Bellamy thought of Luke, "love how the town is steady, reliable. And some people," she thought of Olivia, "Are so excited about the new features, like the theater."

"I actually think that could work. I could do a bread that's based on the history of the town, we could do something, maybe the sign, maybe something else, for the cake. And yeah, let's keep an open mind on the cookie designs. I think it's more important that they look good than that they're creative."

"Two hundred and fifty thousand dollars is going to require them to be both, Clare." Bellamy set aside the flour container and moved on to the sugar. "Just an idea...we have time before we need to be totally settled."

"Two weeks, Bellamy. We have two and half weeks." Clare pulled the donut trays from the racks and motioned Bellamy over. "Okay, now here's how you're going to dip these to glaze them while I finish up the pie crust."

Three hours and four dozen orange-ginger glazed donuts sold later, Bellamy stood at the counter of

Nothin' but Sugar sketching cookie designs between customers.

The bell over the door jingled.

Bellamy looked up, her helpful-bakery-assistant-smile in place. It immediately morphed into a real smile. "Hey there."

"Hey, Bells." Luke returned her smile. "Thought I might find you here."

"Oh?" She tucked her pencil behind her ear, leaning on the counter with both elbows. "What can I get you?"

Luke scanned the glass display case, then asked, "What'd you help make today?"

"Donuts, pie crust, some kind of lemony muffin, and several questionable decisions," she ticked off on her fingers as she answered.

Luke's eyebrows raised. "What kind of questionable decisions?"

"Mostly design related, but also Adrien suckered me into a decorating project next Wednesday and I'm regretting confirming via text this morning."

"Well, I would be more than happy to lighten the load and help you guys with the decorating. Adrien's house or Clare's?"

"You would? That'd be amazing, it will be so much faster. It's actually Mom and Jonathon's house." Having an arborist who climbed trees regularly helping to hang lights truly would make the job faster, but

Bellamy was more pleased at another opportunity to spend time with Luke.

"Sure. I'm always happy to help you, Bells." He returned to studying the display case. "I'll try one of those lemon muffins you mentioned."

"You want it in a box or a bag?"

"I'll just take a napkin, it's not going to last past the walk back to the truck, so let's save some trees."

Bellamy snagged a muffin in a napkin and passed it across to him. His fingers brushed hers, and lingered for a long moment, their eyes meeting. Luke drew in a deep breath before pulling his hand back slowly, his eyes never leaving hers.

He cleared his throat, and breaking the moment, looked down at the sketches next to the register. "Are these the design ideas you were considering bad decisions?"

Bellamy studied his face, noticing the slight flush along his collar. "Yeah."

"They're good." He pointed to one. "This is the old Sand and Sun Inn, by the lighthouse."

"You could tell?"

"It looks just like it. Man, that place is iconic. You making postcards to send to your boyfriend back in LA?"

Bellamy grinned. He'd asked that almost too casually. "I, um, I don't have a boyfriend." When she caught his gaze again, it was the first time she felt as if maybe the power balance in the relationship had shifted. She wasn't some little girl with an unattainable crush. "I'm trying out ideas for the cookie designs."

"Huh. I'm intrigued." He looked at his phone. "Look, I was wondering if you'd have some time to go for a cup of coffee later?"

Bellamy shuddered. "I cannot have any more caffeine today, my heart will simply stop working."

Luke nodded. "Got it. Okay, well, I'm sure I'll see you around."

"Oh! I mean, I didn't mean I didn't want to go out of the shop with you to, you know, somewhere." Bellamy fumbled, grabbing the pencil from behind her ear and twirling it around her fingers, trying to look much more casual than she felt.

"I see." He put a hand out and stilled the pencil, brushing his thumb over the back of her hand before pulling away, leaving a trail of heat. "Can I come back around after the shop closes around two?"

"That would be great."

Chapter Twelve

"Come on, you annoying piece of plastic jerk!" Bellamy growled at the food-safe mylar plastic she was trying to cut into a stencil. Angry, she chucked the sheet as hard as she could at the wall and then watched as it floated ineffectually to the floor.

"Take a break." Clare looked up from the open office door where she was tallying the day's sales and keeping the books before starting the prep for tomorrow's baking.

"It's just so annoying. Tiny little lights, tiny little icicles, tiny, tiny, tiny details, and this thing keeps bending and folding and it's messing up my cuts."

"You're not going to get anything done in this state. Besides, you've been here for almost eleven hours, you should grab a nap before we do some work on the contest recipes."

Bellamy glanced up at the clock. Almost two! She shoved her project pieces back into the plastic container and tossed the ruined mylar sheet into the trash. "Yeah, I think I'll take a walk. Good idea." Bellamy didn't know why she didn't want to explain to Clare about her plans with Luke. It just seemed like something different and fragile, something she didn't want to be everybody's business just yet. Not when she herself didn't even know what was happening.

"I'll be here when you get back. We can taste test some things, that'll be more fun." Clare called as Bellamy headed to the front of the bakery.

She darted outside just as Luke's truck pulled up to the curb.

He rolled down the window and called, "Wanna go for a drive?"

"You know, I could really use a walk right now."

"I've got the perfect place, hop in."

Bellamy climbed up, and he pulled smoothly away, taking them over toward the bay.

After a moment, he asked, "Maybe I'm imagining things, but you seem a bit...salty. Everything okay?"

She huffed out a breath. "It's this decorating thing. I feel like I have to get it right or my idea won't work and if my idea won't work, then we don't win the contest and Clare can't do the next stage of her renovation." Bellamy shook her head, staring out the window as they passed the domed township hall building. "I thought I could treat it like fabric, but it just keeps bending and cracking."

"Sounds like you're putting a lot of pressure on yourself for something that's brand new to you."

Bellamy pushed the heat vent to angle it away from her, still feeling hot from her earlier anger. "It's just, for once I want to win at something that matters. I want to get this right."

Luke was quiet for a moment as they passed the row of bed and breakfasts along the lakeshore drive. "Is this a moment where you want to vent, and I just listen, or a moment where you want help problem-solving?"

"What?" Bellamy blinked at him.

"It's a Gia and Lucy thing. When they call, a lot of times they just want to vent, and they don't, and I quote, 'need a man to fix their problems' for them. They just need somebody to listen, and that helps them come to their own conclusions."

"Wow. Gia told you that?"

"Well," he shrugged, turning down the heat dial and adding, "It was really more Lucy. Gia's been kind of touchy in her pregnancy."

Bellamy laughed. "You're a good brother, you know? I can't picture Adrien ever responding like that."

Luke pulled into a small lot at the end of the row of inns and turned to her before unbuckling his seatbelt. "Can I ask you a favor? Can we, just for right now, pretend that Adrien doesn't exist?"

"Because it's awkward?" Bellamy held her breath, waiting for his answer.

He nodded. "Because it's awkward. Look, I think we both know there's something...different...this time. And, I'd like to explore it. I'd like to have a chance to figure out who you are in a context that's not as my friend's little sister."

"You know we can't exist in a bubble."

"For today, let's try. Just an experiment. To see what happens when all the outside stuff is gone, and it's just us."

"This sounds complicated." Bellamy didn't want to say no, but she wasn't sure that 'yes' was the right answer either.

"Let's make it uncomplicated." Luke offered a soft smile. "And, if we need to, we can untangle it when the time comes."

As if on cue, a golden beam of sunlight pushed through the gray clouds, setting the small ripples on Lake Michigan to twinkling like the Christmas lights starting to be hung around town.

"Okay." She climbed out of the truck. "Now where are we walking to?"

He met her around the front of the vehicle, taking her hand in his. "This trail has been here for a few years, but it started getting popular this summer." He led her past the beach with frozen sand and toward a dirt path framed by two wooden posts at the edge of the woods.

"I thought it was state-owned land and couldn't be built on." Bellamy breathed in the earthy pine scent, the tension from the long day releasing from her shoulders.

"It took a while but there was a petition for land use management to allow for safer, more established hiking trails. This is one of them." He tapped his fingertips along her knuckles where their hands were interlaced. "I actually was part of the team that cleared this trail."

Bellamy studied his profile as they walked. "Impressive. How did you know you wanted to be an arborist?"

He ran his other hand lightly long the needles of the pines edging the trail as he answered, "I just couldn't stand the idea of sitting behind a desk all day. It's fine for some. But, I would rot away piece by piece. Even as a kid, my parents had to drag Gia and me inside for bed on those long summer nights. Honestly, we spent half the summer camping in the backyard because it wasn't worth the fight for them." He chuckled. "I didn't know what I wanted to be; I just knew what I didn't want to be. And then I explored my options. How about you? Did you always want to be a model manager?"

"You know, no. I mean, we all know I wanted to be an actress. Part of me still does." She shrugged, kicking a pinecone down the trail ahead of them. "But the thing is. I was good at it. Managing people, organizing the chaos and keeping things on schedule. I loved the clothes." She swung his hand in the air and twirled under it. "Oh, the clothes were so beautiful."

"A beautiful woman that loves beautiful things." He pulled her into another twirl before steering down the left branch when the trail forked. "This place, you'll love."

"Oh?" She couldn't decide if his comment was sweet or corny. Or maybe it was both. Like this was a secret date, but also it was an experiment. Sometimes things didn't have to be labeled, just enjoyed.

"So this," he ducked and led her through a tunnel through thick pine branches woven together with age, "is why this trail became popular."

She followed him out of the dense greenery and into an open field. There, in the center of the browned husks of wildflowers gone to seed for the season, was an enormous pine tree.

He let go of her hand and turned to her. "This tree became *the* spot to take social media photos." He leaned closer, cupping her cheek with one hand, his green eyes steady. "Imagine this tree, surrounded by a field of wildflowers, birds chirping, a picnic basket, and a checkered blanket."

Bellamy placed a hand on his chest, her other hand reaching up of its own accord to draw his head down nearer to hers. "It sounds lovely."

"It is." His other hand cupped her cheek, and he drew in closer, his eyes now locked onto her lips.

Bellamy felt his heart racing to match her own rushing rhythm as she pulled him in just a little more, closing the gap between them.

His lips brushed hers, feather soft, barely a touch.

"Call From Clare," the mechanical voice on her phone blared into the quiet forest.

Wordlessly, they sprang apart, a small groan sounding from Luke.

"Call from Clare," blared again.

"I, um." Bellamy was breathless, still feeling the tingle of his lips on hers. "I'd better answer that."

Luke nodded and stepped away, his hand in his jean's pockets.

"Hi, Clare!" Bellamy chirped brightly into the phone.

"Hey, just checking in. You've been on your walk for a while. You cooled down?"

"Yeah," Bellamy lied. She was anything but calm and cool, but for a whole different reason now.

"Good. Can you head back, I have an idea, and I think I figured out the way to make the theming work. How far did you walk?"

"Not too far, just a little walk." It wasn't technically a lie.

"Do you need me to come pick you up?"

"Nope, nope. I'll be back soon."

She hung up the phone and shoved it into her back pocket.

"She needs you back at the bakery?" Luke studied her from a few feet away, the spell broken.

"Yeah. I'm sorry."

"Nah, nothin' to be sorry about." His grin was boyish as he added, "Best walk I've had in a while. We have plenty of time for another in the future."

A laugh burst out of Bellamy. "Yeah, it was really nice. Next time I'll put my phone on silent."

"That's a plan I could get behind." He gestured for her to go first through the pine-bough tunnel, placing a hand softly on her lower back as they walked through the quiet woods.

"Listen, Bells—"

"Nope." She cut him off, taking his hand in her and swinging it cheerfully between them.

"Nope what?"

"No, we're not going to talk about what happened. We're not at the tangled stage, and I don't want to end up there just yet. I want to enjoy these little moments while we have them."

Luke gave her hand a squeeze. "Okay. I respect that stance. I could use a little holiday magic myself."

"Good." They reached the truck and she climbed in. "Then you're perfectly fine with dropping me off a block from the bakery?"

He climbed into the truck and turned the engine over, shaking his head. "I can't tell if this makes me feel like I'm back in high school in a good way or not...but sure, I'm game."

Chapter Thirteen

Bellamy floated into the bakery, her mind replaying the soft brush of Luke's lips on her own. If the barest touch had been so wonderful, she could hardly imagine what a real kiss would feel like.

"Earth to Bellamy," Clare called, and based on her expression it might have been the second or third time she'd done so. "Did you get frostbitten? Maybe hypothermic?" Clare was, of course, being sarcastic, as the weather had been in the high forties all day, having jumped back up unexpectedly. Typical of Michigan weather, everybody had clothing layers stashed in their cars and shucked them as needed.

"Oh, sorry." Bellamy hoped the flush in her cheeks was just mistaken for exertion and a bit of chill. "What's the new idea?"

Clare continued to study her with the Mother Bear look for a long moment before beckoning Bellamy through the swinging door and into the kitchen. "This," she stated definitively, waving her arm grandly to showcase a single baked item sitting on a kitchen towel.

Bellamy stared at the slice, studded through with gem-like pieces of fruit, in horror. "Fruitcake? Fruitcake is your big idea?" She bit her lip to stop a tirade of how the hideous dessert was essentially the laughing stock of the holidays. Had Clare buckled under the pressure?

"What?" Clare looked from the sliced bread on the plate to her sister, and back again. "That's not fruitcake." She tore off a piece and held it up to Bellamy to look at it in the light. "Do you see how airy this piece is? It's not even cake."

Bellamy had to admit that she could see the light easily through the slice. It *did* look a lot more like bread than cake. "Okay, then what is it?"

"You really don't remember Grandpa's stollen bread?" She popped the piece she was holding into her mouth and gestured for Bellamy to try a piece as well.

"No," Bellamy answered slowly, pulling a small piece off the edge. It had a nice crust, with a little bit of icing on it. "I was only five when he passed. You were thirteen and already loving being in the kitchen helping." She popped the piece into her mouth. Chewy, crispy, sweet, and spicy, the flavors exploded in her mouth. "Is that...that little extra warmth after the cinnamon, is that alcohol?"

"Rum," Clare answered, "But the one for the contest won't have the after-bake soak, so it won't have as much bite. We'll need the alcohol to all bake off, based on the rules."

"What's inside?" Bellamy pulled off another piece, the spices mixed with a small piece of sugary citrus peel making her think of the oranges their mother always stuffed in the toes of their stockings every Christmas. Maybe some part of her did remember her Grandpa's stollen bread.

"Candied orange and lemon peel. Sometimes I add grapefruit peel too, just to mix it up. Rum-soaked raisins, Grandpa always used both green and red. Rum-soaked almonds. Grandpa used marzipan, so I always add a bit of it, but it can be a strong flavor. And then it's a yeasted dough using milk. Plus warming spices"

"This definitely will be, I think, a unique take on the bread part of the contest." Bellamy pulled up the contest rules she had booked marked on her phone. "But doesn't it take a long time to do the candied peels and soaked stuff?" The spiced flavor of the bread really did speak of the holidays.

Clare nodded, bringing over her recipe book. "It does. But if you look at the rules, each baker can bring up to three pre-made items with them. The stipulation is that the items must be homemade still. I think they know that only a few hours to prep the night before and then less than a day in the kitchen for the actual contest will be too short for three totally different types of items. At least, if they want them to be both TV worthy and taste good."

Bellamy found the fine print and it did confirm what Clare had said. "Okay. So if we do this bread, how do we tie it all together?"

Clare held up a finger, flipping through the recipe book. "Good question. So, you're more of a story-teller. Honest opinion on if this works. Back in the day, Treeview had a lot of German and Bohemian settlers. Stollen is a German recipe." She found the page she was looking for. "And then the fur trappers and traders that came were often French. So, I was thinking for the cake, I can make a crêpe cake."

"Do we really want to celebrate people that set-tled land that wasn't theirs?" Bellamy thought of the social media aspect for advertising Nothin' But Sugar afterward, and the history of what settlement looked like.

"Here's the thing." Clare tapped the recipe book as she searched for words. "It's not celebrating the act of settling. It's more about celebrating the way that cultures and food blend together in a modern-day melting pot. Food is family. You said you wanted to highlight Treeview. So, let's highlight the foods that built this town into what it is today."

Bellamy nodded. "Okay. I mean, I get it. But how do we tie it together with flavor?"

"Easy, the warming spices. I'll do a cinnamon filling for the crêpe cake. We can add a hint of warming spices to the cookies. Maybe a bit of lemon or orange zest. It will tie it all together without being too similar. Plus," Clare tapped the recipe book again as she said, "it will really show off a variety of techniques, without me competing head-to-head with skilled traditional cake bakers."

"Smart." Bellamy beamed at her older sister. They really had a shot to win this thing with this type of creative thinking. The butterflies that had been dancing in her stomach since her kiss slowly settled into a hard ball. "So, you're part is down—"

"It's still going to take practice to make sure I can do it fast enough and neat enough."

"Fair. But, we still have got to nail down the cookies." Bellamy eyed the container with her decorating supplies, fighting against the self-doubt whispering inside her. "I need to buckle down on that. Do you like the building idea? We can have them decorated for the holidays."

"I do really like the idea. I was thinking about what buildings would be right for it. I love the idea of the Sun and Sand Inn and the lighthouse. What about Klein's Tavern? It's pretty historic looking."

Bellamy pulled up the search page on her cell phone. "Yep. Established in eighteen eighty-three, it says. I'd say that's pretty historic." She took a screenshot of the photo of the Tavern, pushing down the tightness clenching in her chest.

Clare's phone vibrated, shaking the metal prep table it was on.

"It's a text from Kev. He says dinner will be ready in an hour." Clare moved a ribbon in the recipe book to mark her page and walked over to shove the thick book into her shoulder bag. "We should head out. Olivia's back in school tomorrow and between homework and rehearsals, we'll barely see the poor thing except for meals."

Bellamy nodded, still scrolling through an article about a historic walking tour of Treeview that operated in the summer and early fall. "Okay, yeah. Let's take the night off and then tomorrow is a deep dive into decorating practice."

"Agreed. I'll be working on my crepe technique all week, so I hope you're hungry for blintzes and crêpes for breakfast every day."

Chapter Fourteen

The next few days flew past. By day, Bellamy practiced flooding cookies with icing and using piping to create pools to divide the cookies into sections. She airbrushed paper towels and practice cookies and discarded crêpes that she and Clare later ate for lunch. Each break was punctuated with photo texts to Luke of her work and his return texts, usually involving squirrels doing cute things or one time a porcupine staring him down from midway up a Jack Pine.

Each night, she woke up in a cold sweat, plagued by anxiety. So much of her time in Treeview felt too good to be true. Dreams punctuated by all of her cookies looking like a kindergartener decorated them, or of her slipping and dropping the entire plate while walking to the judging table woke her at almost exactly two in the morning each day.

Wednesday was the same, only this time she was in the forest, looking for a cake. She was carrying a sack of cookies and she had the airbrush in her hands, and she kept painting bubble after bubble in the snow. Despite the fact that her half-awake rational brain knew the airbrush needed to be plugged in, that it wasn't possible, and that Clare was in charge of the cake, Bellamy woke up gasping for air, her heart pounding.

With a groan, she pulled on thick socks and padded out into the kitchen. Moving softly, so as not to wake her sleeping family upstairs, Bellamy pulled a glass from the cupboard and filled it from the tap.

She sipped the water between deep breaths, using the technique she'd walked many models through during the past few years. Deep breaths. Work through it. What was the problem? Usually for the models it was something obvious, like a schedule conflict or a barking photographer. Sometimes a break-up or a really cruddy comment on a photo online.

"Triage it, Bellamy," she whispered to herself. What had been the worst part of the dream? The searching. The panic about not finding the cake. "Okay, but what does the cake represent?" She finished her water and headed back to the office-turned-bedroom. The deep breathing had worked to loosen the vice-like grip on her lungs.

Settling back into the futon, she checked her phone. Maybe there would be a cute message from Luke, who often stayed up later than she did with her current bakery schedule. No message. But the icon for her email had a red dot, indicating an unread message.

When she opened the app, she saw four new messages. Two were junk. One was a casting call for a small speaking role, no agent needed. The last was from one of the apartments she'd found in her last early morning ad comb-through. Skimming the email, she saw that yes, there was a room available. She would need to share a bathroom with one of the other three roommates. The rent was certainly reasonable, and if she got even a quarter of the winnings from the baking contest, she could spend the first few months auditioning and getting the licensing and connections for her own model managing company without stressing about a job.

At the end of the email the apartment owner, who had CC'd the other renter, asked if she could complete a video interview before the end of December. Bellamy responded with a quick yes and offered a few days between the Christmas In Town Square weekend and Christmas day.

"There." She let out a deep breath. "Now you can stop searching. You will have a place to live when you go back." She shoved her hair out of her face as she scrunched down into the covers. "Now, focus on the contest. You can do this." She repeated the mantra over and over as she fell back asleep.

Adrien pulled up to the bakery in his jeep and waved to Bellamy through the window.

See you soon! She texted Luke before slinging on her coat and calling out to Clare, "I'm off to decorate Mom's house! Adrien'll drop me off at your place after."

She heard Clare's affirmative response from the back, where she was prepping the dough for tomorrow's bakes.

Can't wait. Her phone showed her Luke's response as she closed the bakery door behind her, making sure the bells were positioned to jingle for Clare should a customer go in. Giddy, Bellamy gave Adrien a big grin as she slid into the passenger seat.

"Hey, bro. Let's decorate!"

Adrien grunted in amusement. "Somebody's a ray of California sunshine today."

"You know it." She flipped down the sun visor, checking her makeup.

"Ah, there's the little princess I used to fight over the bathroom with before school every day." Adrien turned up the radio, Kenny G's instrumental Christmas album piping through the jeep's speakers.

Bellamy stuck her tongue out at him, scrunching up her nose.

Before long, they were pulling up behind Luke's truck in the winding drive to their childhood home.

"Hey guys." Luke nodded to them both, winking at Bellamy when Adrien turned to open the hatch of the jeep.

"Hi." Bellamy met his wink with a warm smile, rehatching the butterflies tickling her heart.

Adrien dragged out a box with a giant inflatable snowman inside. "I got this new one, I think it will crack Jonathon and Mom up. Bellamy, can you go get the spare key and open the garage? They've got the lights and extension cords in the plastic tubs under the workbench. Luke and I will get the ladder set up." He gestured to the extension ladder that was nearly ever-present in the bed of Luke's truck.

"Sure," Bellamy agreed. "Is the key in the usual spot?"

"Yep, third dog statue over, like always."

Bellamy snuck a glance behind her to watch as Luke easily lifted the ladder from the truck bed. He caught her looking and flashed a grin before turning to reply to something Adrien said. It didn't take her long to find the key, and after fitting it into the lock and opening the garage door, she pulled her gloves and fleece headband from her coat pockets and slipped them on. The cold snap had returned with a vengeance. No snow, just bitter wind.

By the time she'd found the three tubs of lights and extension cords, with the waterproof timer and two small wire-lit snowmen, the ladder had been set up at the corner of the house and the inflatable snowman unboxed.

"Bells, can you grab us an extension cord?" Luke called, breaking down the box for easier storage.

"Got it!" She opened the dark green tub and pulled out an orange extension cord, joining them in the middle of the yard.

"No, we should use the green cords, they'll blend in better." Adrien frowned at the safety-orange cord.

"It's just going to be covered in snow anyhow," Bellamy continued to hold the cord out to him.

"It doesn't always snow that much by Christmas Eve, you know." Adrien held his hands up refusing to take the cord.

"Here," Luke interrupted their bickering, taking the orange cord and tossing it toward the ladder. "How about Bellamy and I take stock of the lights, and you figure out how you want to run the power?"

"Yeah, good call. I'll start from the side outlet and see how many green versus orange cords Jonathon has here." Adrien strutted off to the first bin, leaving Bellamy and Luke behind.

"My hero," Bellamy teased.

"I just figured giving him a solo project would give me the chance to do this." Luke leaned in and brushed a quick kiss on her cheek. "Which is still a lot less than I'd like to be doing right now."

"Oh?" Bellamy's heart quickened, her body aching to lean in and finally feel how many fireworks a real kiss would light up inside her.

"Hey!" Adrien called.

They snapped apart.

"Quit lollygagging and start untangling lights," He added, his upper body halfway in the tub of decorations searching for extension cords.

Bellamy laughed nervously, leading the way over to the tubs beside her older brother. It really did feel a lot like high school keeping their budding relationship in a secretive bubble. Only now, instead of her trying to find ways to get included to be near Luke, he was also seeking time with her.

As they sorted through the bins, pulling out multi-colored lights and long tangled strands of icicle lights, Bellamy found herself brushing up against Luke. Even though their winter coats and gloves dampened the spark, the moments were playful and fun.

It was just the lighthearted break from reality that she needed. Each time Luke's eyes met hers, or they pulled apart just to come together again as they spread strings of decorations across the yard, the little glow of happiness in her chest brightened. Luke's eyes were dancing with merriment, and the grin he'd had since he'd kissed her cheek seemed plastered in place.

"Okay, we're ready to start hanging." Adrien returned from where he'd been laying out a web of power cords. "Snowman first." He jogged over to where the nylon of the limp snowman was wafting in the wind, held in place only by the stakes Adrien and Luke had pounded into the cold earth while Bellamy was in the garage earlier.

They all whooped and cheered as Adrien inserted the plug and flipped the switch, the motor pumped air in, slowly bringing the giant decoration to its full six-foot height.

"I think it might be a bit of an abomination," Bellamy laughed, leaning into Luke.

"I believe you're thinking of the Yeti," Luke replied, draping an arm over her shoulder.

Adrien looked away from his prized decoration and his brows drifted down. "Alright, that's done. The game isn't over, that's not even halftime. Luke,

I assume you want to climb? I'll hand you the lights, and Bellamy you stay on tangle-duty."

Bellamy frowned at her brother. She had the distinct feeling he was inserting himself between her and Luke with his assignments intentionally.

It didn't take long to confirm that she was right. Within minutes of Luke scaling the ladder, Adrien beckoned her closer.

"What?" She blinked innocently at her brother.

"What are you doing?" Adrien kept his voice low enough that Luke wouldn't be able to hear them.

"Decorating Mom's house, what are you doing?" She replied obstinately.

"Bellamy. Why are you getting involved with anybody while you're here? Let alone Luke?" Adrien braced the ladder with one hand, and when he turned to look up and verify that Luke had enough slack in the light string, Bellamy could see the muscle in his jaw ticking.

"Why do you care? We have an understanding, and we're both adults."

The ladder clanged as Luke started his descent. "Let's move it about two feet down." If he sensed the tension in the air, he ignored it as he focused on re-setting the ladder safely.

When he'd ascended again, Adrien turned back to Bellamy. "I don't think you have the same understanding."

"We do. Not that it's any of your business, but we agreed that we'd untangle the tricky stuff when it came time. That we could just exist in a bubble of exploring this for right now." The soft warmth that had kept her feeling so light all day started to dim. The searching. The bubbles from her dream. Her heart sank further when Adrien swiped a gloved hand down his face.

"Look," He frowned as he continued, "I think maybe I need to come clean about something."

"What?" Bellamy kept her face and voice carefully neutral.

The string of lights beside them was hauled up the ladder, tinkling lightly as it rubbed and bumped against the metal.

"You're going to be mad."

"Tell me." She stared him down.

The regret was clear in his brown eyes as he said, "I may have given people the impression that you're going to be home for a while." He held up both hands in a gesture of peace before gripping the ladder sides again.

"You did what?" Bellamy fought to keep her voice low. "Why? How?"

The ladder bounced as Luke clambered down again. This time he studied them both with concern. When neither offered any information, he shook his head. "Let's move down another few feet. We're almost done, so if you two could stay civil, that'd be good."

Bellamy forced a chuckle and Adrien wordlessly helped Luke move the ladder.

Once Luke was back to work clipping lights to the gutter, Adrien said softly, "I think it's best we have this conversation in the truck after."

Bellamy stared him down, fuming. "I need to know exactly what you said." Had Luke only been spending time with her out of pity? Poor failure Bellamy. Let's cheer her up with some ice skating.

"Yes. I owe you that. Let's just finish this up and we can talk about it in the truck. Before you and Luke move past this flirting." He paused, studiously not looking at her. "Please tell me it's only been flirting."

"It has." Bellamy seethed, unzipping her coat and letting the brisk wind cool her off.

Three more trips up and down the ladder and a layer of warm white icicle lights dripped across the front of the house. Strung alongside that was a single row of multicolor lights.

"Look, I don't know what's going on here." Luke gestured between them both as he collapsed the ladder. "But whatever it is, it's nothing that can't be untangled." He looked at Bellamy as he said that, his green eyes warm and gentle. He turned to Adrien, "I started it, so whatever you have to say about it, you can say it to me."

"No." Bellamy shook her head. "We can talk about it later. Adrien has a few explanations he owes me." She dumped the extra light strings and extension cords unceremoniously into the tub before stacking it inside the two empty ones. She stomped away, dragging the tubs into the garage.

Adrien was talking softly to Luke, gesturing animatedly when she finished returning the spare key. Luke shot her a look, then shrugged.

"Call me later," Luke said, leaning in to pull her into a tight hug. "Go easy on him, tiger."

Bellamy choked out a half-laugh and pulled away, holding up a hand in a wave as she stalked to the passenger side of the jeep and slammed the door.

When Adrien climbed in, she turned to him, "What exactly have you been telling people about my personal business?" She snapped out each word, dreading the response.

Adrien started the jeep and backed out, waving to Luke as his pickup pulled out behind them and headed in the other direction.

"Adrien." Bellamy hissed.

"It's not what you think." He turned down the saxophone crooning out *Silent Night* and shrugged. "I thought I was helping. That first morning in the bakery, it seemed like half the town asked you when you'd gotten in and when you were leaving. And I know you tried to be nonchalant, but your smile faltered or your shoulders slumped just a little bit more each time. And that was only in the half hour or so it took me to do the windows."

Bellamy groaned. "So, you decided to what? To go ahead and tell everybody I came home broke and jobless and would be spending the rest of my twenties sleeping on the futon in my older sister's husband's office?"

"No." Adrien's voice rose to compete with Bellamy's. "That is not what I did."

"Okay, then what exactly, and I do mean exactly, did you say?"

"I may have indicated to several people, and Luke happened to be among them, that you didn't have a set plan to leave. I made it sound good. Like you're on sabbatical from a stressful job. The kind that you can't disclose a lot about. Made it sound fancy."

Bellamy dropped her head into her hands. "So you lied?"

"No," Adrien hedged, pulling into Clare's driveway and putting the jeep in park. "It's more that I hinted here and there and allowed Natalia Clancy to develop her own version of the truth."

"Natalia Clancy?" Bellamy groaned, keeping her head safely buried. "By now half the town probably thinks I worked for some giant star and caught them cheating or something else scandalous and got exiled." She pressed the palms of her hands to her eyes to stem the tears. "But more important-ly...Luke thinks I'm here for...well, maybe for good? Maybe for an undisclosed extremely long amount of time?"

Adrien cleared his throat. "Uh. Yeah. That's why I needed to talk to you."

Bellamy pulled her head out of her hands and turned to face him, her heart dropping. The bubble of unreality for her had meant ignoring that they would end up facing a long-distance relationship. The bubble of uncomplicated for Luke had meant that they could figure out their attraction before involving their families. They'd gone into their first kiss with two entirely different ideas of what keep-ing it uncomplicated meant.

She swallowed hard. "And that's why you said we have different understandings."

Adrien rubbed the back of his neck, staring out the windshield. "Yeah."

"You set me up to be another Alice." Bellamy's stomach churned. She was an idiot. They'd even talked about how Treeview was the only place Luke ever saw himself living. "And I selfishly ignored reality and thought we could play pretend, just for a little while. Until we had to make a decision."

"Look, I didn't know this," Adrien gestured be-tween her and air, "was going to happen. I don't think even Luke expected it."

Bellamy nodded once, curtly. "Of course not. Who could have expected him to like me?"

"That's not what I mean." Adrien frowned at her. "Despite that. Whatever it is, just end it. End it before it does hurt. He doesn't deserve another Alice." He drummed his hands on the top of the steering wheel. "She hurt him bad, Bellamy."

"I know." She answered quietly, thinking of what Clare had told her about the break-up.

He cleared his throat again. "Look, it's early. It will be awkward, sure. But nobody's feelings will be destroyed, yet. So pull the plug."

"Yeah." Bellamy nodded numbly, putting her hand on the door handle and tugging it. "It's still early enough, everybody will be fine." She pushed the door open and slid out of the seat before Adrien could see the tears gathering in her eyes.

If that was true, why did it feel like her heart was breaking?

Chapter Fifteen

"So that's why you came back." Luke sat beside her on the steps of Clare's house, watching the sun slide behind the trees.

"Yeah." Bellamy pushed her hands deeper into her coat pockets, hunching over her own knees. "Pretty embarrassing, huh?"

"I gotta admit that the story Adrien and Natalia concocted between the two of them with their half-truths was more exciting." Even though they were sitting right next to each other, they were carefully not touching.

"Look, Luke, I'm really sorry. I feel like if I'd thought even a little bit, and not just been giddy and excited, I would have clarified the uncomplicated thing more." She yearned to inch over to her left and press into him, let his strength soothe her after being so vulnerable. But she wouldn't.

He shook his head, looking at her for the first time since she'd finished her story. His eyes were soft and clear. "Nah. Like I said to Adrien, I started it. Last I checked, it takes two to tango."

"I guess I just got...well, you know. It's no secret I had such a crush on you when you were a senior and I was a freshman." She smiled ruefully at him. After explaining everything that had happened with Amma and her desperate attempt to find a job, this truth felt much easier to admit.

He raised an eyebrow. "Only that one year?"

Bellamy clucked her tongue on the top of her mouth. "Oh come on now."

Luke chuckled. "It's a fair question. I admit that I didn't see you as anything more than a kid then. But it didn't take too many years for that to change. Course, by then you were already gone more than you were here."

"Really?" She sat up straighter and angled her body toward his. "I never had a clue."

"You sure?" He shrugged, propping one elbow on a knee to face her as well. "I almost made a move, too, friendships and consequences be damned."

She raised her eyebrows in disbelief.

"I did. Remember that first summer you came home? Clare's bakery had just opened, and Olivia was turning five. So you came home for the fourth of July and all the celebrations."

"Yeah, I remember..." She trailed off thinking back. "That was when we had that huge mess because Adrien dropped a fifty-pound sack of flour. It exploded everywhere."

"And conveniently Adrien had to take a call in the middle of cleaning it up." Luke nodded. "So it was just you and I scrambling to get the bakery back to its normal state before Clare got back. You had your hair up, you looked so good in that little blue dress, but you kept sliding around in those dark blue heels on the flour."

Bellamy groaned. "Oh my gosh, I forgot about the heels! I never did get the flour out of that satin. Terrible choice of outfit for bakery work."

Luke laughed, "I have noticed you've been a lot more practical this time around. Anyhow...you'd gotten flour streaked across your face, and I leaned in to clean it up."

"Oh my gosh, I remember that! I thought for a minute you were going to kiss me."

"I almost did."

She bit her lower lip. "Why didn't you?"

He tilted his head. "Do you not remember your boyfriend walking through the door and you throwing yourself into his arms?"

"Oh. Yeah." She had forgotten, actually. "Parker." She waved a hand through the air, dismissing her ex. "That was his grand gesture, showing up to surprise me after we'd had a big fight. One of many. We broke up for good like a month later, back in LA."

"Well, that's why I didn't make a move."

She nodded and gave a soft sigh. "I wish he hadn't shown up."

"You still would've gone back to LA." He turned forward again, clasping his hands together, one elbow on each knee. "Though, then, the idea of long distance wasn't as daunting."

Bellamy's heart sank. The next time she'd visited home, he'd been with Alice. "Yeah, I guess I would have left. I loved the city so much back then."

"Seems to me you're still planning to go back now." He didn't turn to look at her as he said, "Do you still love it?"

Bellamy pushed her hat lower as the wind gusted through. "I don't know. I used to love the lights and the parties and that everybody had some kind of exciting story." She hunched back down, retreating into her coat as the last of the orange sunlight faded into the shadows. "Now it's like...I just. I need to go back. I need to have made all of that time and effort worth it. I just...I need to."

Luke pressed his lips together, staring off into the trees before answering. "Well. I'd never hold you back. But Bells, I can't do the long distance. Not when there's no end in sight."

She closed her eyes, willing the tears forming to just give her a few more minutes. Just long enough to finish the conversation. "Yeah," she said, her voice thick.

"I would hate to turn this into something angry and bitter." He looked down at his boots, worn and scuffed. 'It's not what I would choose for us. Or for our families."

Opening her eyes, she watched him as he seemed to shutter himself away. "I....yeah." She couldn't apologize again, because even if she never got another chance to kiss him, the past week had been confirmation of what she'd known for years. Luke was kind, and honest, and steady. He was so many things she wanted but didn't deserve.

"So." He stood, and turned to face her. "I'm flying out to Colorado Christmas day. Let's just go radio silence until I get back. Let things sort themselves out, and then by the next time we're in the same room again it might just feel a little more like normal."

Bellamy nodded, not trusting herself to answer him.

With the sun now gone, and the porch light still off, she couldn't see his face as he said, "Merry

Christmas, Bells. See ya in the new Year, if you're still here."

Chapter Sixteen

"It's been a week and I think you need to forgive me." Adrien held out his peace offering of a spinach, cranberry, and walnut salad. "I said I was sorry."

Bellamy reached across the glass bakery counter, now decorated with red tinsel and white Christmas lights along the front edges, and took the offered salad. "I'm not mad at you."

"You've barely responded to my texts." Adrien settled the paper bag on the counter and removed his leather driving gloves. "I know I went too far and shouldn't have said anything. To be fair, I was trying to protect you."

"I've barely responded to anyone's texts." Bellamy popped open the clear container and poured the lemon feta dressing over her lunch. "It's not just you."

He narrowed his eyes, studying her face. "Truth?"

Bellamy nodded, knowing that her big brother was genuinely worried if he was reverting back to their childhood codeword. Better than a pinky promise, and more honest, she responded, "Truth." And it was the truth. She'd fully immersed herself in cookie decorating, only coming up for air to help Olivia and Miss Everly with the costumes on Saturday as she'd promised.

It was also true that she'd been intentionally leaving her cell phone in her purse, or sometimes even back at Clare's house. It was easier to squash the temptation to text Luke. Every time she got a detail right, or figured out a new technique, she wanted to show it to him and see his celebratory texts, or funny animal photos back. It also made it so she wasn't stopping every two minutes to check and see if he'd changed his mind and no longer wanted space. It was the only way she could push down her feelings and focus on what she needed to get done.

"Thanks for the salad." Bellamy didn't want to talk about the miscommunication anymore. It was in the review mirror, where it needed to stay.

"Yeah, no problem. Clare said you guys were getting sick of crêpes, so seemed like the perfect excuse to come check on you."

"I'm a big girl now, Adrien, I don't need you to look out for me."

"Look, I'm your big brother, and if you think I'm going to sit back and—"

"Surely you brought me lunch too," Clare interrupted as she entered from the kitchen.

Bellamy snickered. Clare had spent half her life interrupting their bickering.

"Of course. I might make some bad decisions when it comes to my sisters, but I'm not an idiot." Adrien unpacked two more takeout boxes from the bag on the counter. "How's the contest prep going?"

Clare made quick work of prepping her own salad as she answered, "It's going surprisingly well. Doncha think so, Bellamy?"

Bellamy nodded, crunching through her salad, deeply relieved to be eating something fresh and green. "Yeah, I think we're in as good a spot as we'll get." She'd finally mastered the airbrush and figured out that it was easier to create the miniature holiday decorations on acetate sheets before using tweezers to get them perfectly in place.

"Man, we need to make sure we both record it so Mom and Jonathon can watch it when they get back." Adrien bit into his wrap.

"Oh, speaking of Mom," Bellamy put her fork down to grab her purse, digging to the bottom to unearth her phone. "Why does Mom think I'm still in California?" She held up the latest text from their mother, which showed Jonathon relaxing on a beach. Beneath it, her mom had written a silly note about how they were pretending they were celebrating the holiday season in the same weather as Bellamy.

Clare and Adrien exchanged glances, then both shrugged.

"We didn't want to get her hopes up that you'd be here when they get home. You know, since you haven't specified exactly when you're leaving."

"Plus we didn't want her to worry about you on her vacation," Clare said around a mouthful of spinach.

"I'm more shocked that she didn't hear it from the rumor mill," Adrien added.

"Or from you." Clare looked pointedly at Bellamy. "You can't stay mad at Adrien for answering people's questions about you when you, yourself aren't communicating to the people you should."

"Hey!" Bellamy dropped her phone back in her purse and gestured at Clare with her fork. "I already said I'm not mad anymore. Plus, maybe I selflessly didn't want Mom to worry either. Hmmm, Clare Clare the Mother Bear?" Granted, it had been more that she didn't want to tell her mom about her failures until she had a new plan in place.

"Okay, okay, okay. Bellamy's not mad at me, and Mom will get the delightful surprise of having all three of her children here for Christmas. It's a win-win." Adrien pulled his phone out and brought up the Christmas in Town Square event schedule. "Before I forget, I wanted to check-in with you on the plans. Friday will be packed. I know Kev is on Olivia duty, but where can I help out?"

Clare crowded in to look at the schedule. "Yeah, it's going to be tight." She pointed to the timeline as she spoke. "So, Belly and I will need to be in the contest kitchen tomorrow night for the three hours of prep and orientation, and then it re-opens for us the next morning, Friday, at eight in the morning."

"Yes! We finally get to sleep in," Bellamy joked. Between the contest prep and keeping up with the regular orders at the bakery, both she and Clare had been up by four every day.

Clare glanced briefly up at her then continued, "So, the contest judging is the part that that's live, the rest will be trimmed and cut for the special later. That's at four-thirty. The show opens at six-thirty, so I should be able to get there on time, but it'll be tight." She paused. "You know what, it would be perfect if you could do the floral run. Kev is picking Olivia up from school and taking her to dinner and then the theater."

Adrien nodded. "Yeah, easy. What do you want? Be specific, because flowers are not the thing you want left up to me."

"I'll call the order in. Be prepared, we're going big. It's Olivia's first community theater production, so I want to make it special."

"Thanks for coming and helping again, Aunty Baa Baa." Olivia was absolutely giddy with excitement as she led Bellamy into The Pine before the first of two planned dress rehearsals. "I know Miss Everly is so grateful too."

Bellamy followed behind her, more than a little worried about how chaotic this first dress rehearsal would be with so many cast members and several costume changes for many of them. "It's no problem."

Olivia beamed as she stopped in front of the red door. "My first time in a real dress rehearsal! This is, like, so totally amazing!" She pulled Bellamy into a quick hug before disappearing into the women's dressing room.

Bellamy grinned and waved. Then she squared her shoulders and prepared to walk into the costuming room.

"Bellamy. Thank goodness, I have about six last-minute alterations that I need your help with, darling." Miss Everly's curly gray hair was even wilder than usual, sticking up in odd places. "And our Tiny Tim is suddenly afraid of wearing makeup and he is simply refusing. Joy is beside herself."

"On it." Bellamy grabbed Tiny Tim's hat and set off to find Joy. The stage manager was doubling as part of the costume and makeup department for the dress rehearsals and opening weekend because many of the crew members were also part of local committees participating in Christmas In Town Square.

It didn't take her long to find Joy backstage, kneeling in front of the young actor, who had his arms stubbornly crossed in front of him. Joy muttered something into her headset and startled when Bellamy knelt beside her.

"Hey, Joseph. I hear you're not into the makeup thing." She gently placed the hat on the little boy's head. "There, that's better."

Joseph swiped the hat off his head. "I'm not doing it!"

"I've tried everything." Joy passed Bellamy the cream makeup palette and sponge. "I even tried bribery with ice cream, but no dice." She paused and listened to something in her headset again. "I gotta go, our director wants a few lighting cues adjusted." She patted Bellamy's shoulder and shot one last exasperated look at Joseph before muttering, "Good luck."

Unphased, Bellamy dabbed the sponge in the makeup as she asked, "So, Joseph. Did you always want to be an actor?"

"No. Not if it means wearing makeup. I didn't know I'd have to."

"Ooookay." Bellamy was getting the distinct feeling that convincing a small child to participate would be a lot like convincing a drunk model that she wasn't networking well at a party. "Well, technically, you don't *have* to wear the makeup. But you might look weird in the lights."

"Like a monster?" He perked up a little, loosening his arms.

"Erm. Well, not exactly. More like...a really cute snowman, because the lights will wash you out."

"I don't want to look cute!" He stomped his foot, and fiercely recrossed his arms. "I'm not a girl, so I don't wear makeup!"

"Ah," Bellamy nodded sagely. "Of course. You know boys can and do wear makeup too."

"No, they don't."

"Mr. Scrooge will. The guy playing your dad in the play will."

"Oh."

Bellamy put down the makeup palette and grabbed the hat again. "Can I put this back on? It's part of your costume. I think, if we have the brim right, we can avoid most of the makeup."

He didn't respond, but he also didn't dodge her when she placed the hat back on his head.

"Here, come out to the stage with me. I need to look at you in the lights." She beckoned him to the edge of the curtain.

He reluctantly followed. "It's too bright."

"Well," Bellamy kept her voice friendly and adjusted the hat lower, "I think we can use the hat to help with that too." She tugged the hat into place, with the brim just slightly askew. "You know, Tiny Tim doesn't really need makeup."

"Good.'

"But he does need a little dirt smudge. How about that? Boys can have dirt smudges, right?"

"Yeah." He nodded.

Bellamy grabbed the makeup sponge and swiped it across his face. "Oh, this is the perfect color for a smudge of dirt." She worked it in along his cheekbone. Between the hat and his refusal, she felt sure they could make just the bare minimum work. "Now, we just need a little here." She dipped the edge of the sponge in the dark brown. "Look up for me, and hold very still." He did as she asked, and she carefully lined his lower lid. "Now, this is the best part of the dirt, because it really makes Tiny Tim look tough. Can you close your eyes for me?"

"Okay. I wanna look tough!"

She quickly lined his upper lid. "Alright, before you go on stage make sure you get some lip balm from Joy." She tapped her lips. "Because Tiny Tim's house is very cold, so his lips are probably always chapped." She patted his shoulder, caught Joy's eye, and gave a thumbs up as she sent him back to stand by his mom.

Back in the costuming room, Miss Everly had a stack of small alterations ready for her. There was a line of actors and actresses in the hall waiting for their garments, each one getting a last-minute look-over from the older woman, with small details and accessories being assigned. Bellamy set to work on the alterations, humming happily to herself. This was exactly the type of chaos she thrived in. For a few minutes, she even forgot about all of the heartache and failure she was carrying around, pushed deep down inside.

Chapter Seventeen

Friday morning brought snowflakes and gentle winds. It also brought nerves and excitement. Bellamy shimmied into her red sequinned designer mini dress and pulled her hair into a slick bun. Highly aware that the bakers and their helpers were being recorded for the full day, she'd gotten up early enough to do her makeup as well.

"Baby Belly, are you ready? We've gotta go." Clare called from just outside the office door.

"Yep." Bellamy cast one last look at the red satin heels waiting by the chair. With a wan smile, she decided she wouldn't risk repeating a flour-spill slip and slide. Pushing Luke out of her head, she stepped into a pair of white sneakers.

"Are you really wearing that to bake in?" Clare herself had on practical green dress slacks and the red chef's coat provided by the contest showrunners.

"What?' Bellamy did a quick twirl. "I wore spandex shorts under it, and I'll have an apron on."

Clare opened her mouth to argue, then looked at her watch and sighed. "Fine. You do you and all that. Let's hit the road."

Bellamy placed the letter she'd written for Olivia to commemorate her opening night on the end table by the door and shrugged into her coat as she followed Clare to the van. Once they were buckled in and backing out, she checked her phone. Two new notifications. One message from Adrien and one missed call from a number she didn't know. Nothing from Luke.

"I sort of like that we're actually going to surprise Mom for once," Bellamy said, watching the windshield wipers shove a line of snowflakes off the vehicle.

Clare chuckled, but it was a tight, nervous sound. "Yeah. She only had to be thousands of miles away and with spotty cell phone service for the three of us to manage it."

"She's going to be so proud of you." Bellamy fought down her own nerves as they drew closer to the luxury summer camp kitchen that the TV station had converted into the set for the contest.

Clare parked the van in the designated area. "She's going to be proud of both of us. But we'll all be a lot happier if we walk out with some money from this. Even if things go sideways, keep trying. Even third place would be a gift."

"Yeah. I will. I won't let you down." Bellamy glanced at the parking area. It looked like about half of the other bakers had arrived based on the five cars parked. "We only have to do better than seven other teams if we want third."

Clare took a deep breath, then nodded sharply. "Let's do this."

They stepped out of the van and closed the doors in unison.

"Wow, that looked like you rehearsed it! Shoot, I wish the cameras had caught that, it would be such as good intro moment." Sharla, the primary production assistant for baker-wrangling called from the door into the kitchen, her ever-present clipboard in hand. "Nothin' But Sugar, right?" She asked as she checked off their names. "You're at the same station as last night, station three. Remember that you cannot go into the walk-ins or touch the bakery racks before the timer starts this morning. You are welcome to walk through the kitchen area and refamiliarize yourself with the space and storage, but, I cannot emphasize this enough, no touching anything. Bakers that start early will be disqualified."

"Thank you, Sharla." Bellamy gave the younger woman a warm smile. She'd worked a few similar temp jobs back in LA when modeling gigs were harder to find, and it was often thankless work.

"You're welcome. You have about ten minutes until role call and instructions."

Inside the enormous room, much had changed from the prior night. Thursday's introduction and prep-bake time would not be included in the TV special aside from some of the baker interviews they did in a small room off to the side. Now, the entire kitchen was illuminated by stage lights, with boom mics placed in strategic locations and large rolling cameras being operated by men and women dressed in black clothing.

"Whoa." Clare swallowed hard. "And I thought the interview room yesterday was intimidating."

"Look, it's a reality-style show, so they're not expecting you to play to camera except when you're being interviewed. Just focus on your work. It's just another day at the bakery, except it's like Thanksgiving on fast-forward."

Clare tore her gaze from the cameras to look at Bellamy in confusion. "That's supposed to be reassuring?"

Bellamy bumped her shoulder into Clare's and put an arm around her for a quick squeeze. "I was in awe of how perfect your timing was for all those pie orders. This will be like nothing compared to that. Just, you know, rely on your list."

"Yeah. Yeah, okay, I can do that." Clare unfolded the list tucked in the pocket of her chef's coat and skimmed down it. "We brought the rum-soaked raisins, right?" She didn't wait for Bellamy to answer before continuing, the very act of checking through her list calming her down. "We also brought the candied citrus peels. Those together made our four pre-prep ingredients."

Bellamy wistfully took in the invigorating controlled frenzy of people prepping the set. It was so much like LA. She shook herself back into focus and went through the list with Clare. They needed to win.

"You did the first round of rest for the yeasted Stollen dough yesterday, so that should be ready to knead in the fruits and nuts." Bellamy added.

"And while I'm doing that, you'll be working on your mini holiday decor on the acetate."

"Yes." Bellamy nodded. She would also be gathering the supplies for Clare to start on the cookie dough while the bread took its second rest and rise.

Before they could rehearse their plan again, Sharla was clapping her hands. "Okay, Bakers!" She called loudly. "I m going to need each of you at your stations. Mixe from the sound crew will come around and place lapel mics on each of you. Once your mic is in place, you will have a hot mic, so be aware. He'll show you how to turn it off for restroom use. We highly recommend doing that."

Clare shot Bellamy a panicked look.

Biting her lip to stop from laughing she whispered, "I promise I will not allow you to use the bathroom with a recording microphone. No matter what else happens today, I will not fail you on that."

Chapter Eighteen

Bellamy puffed the airbrush onto the paper towel beside the cookies, deeply grateful she'd had the good sense to wear sneakers and not heels. The first two hours of the morning had been spent with the film crew orienting the bakers and their assistants to the process of filming. After the director reminded each baker of the rules, the timer for the six hours of baking was started.

"Clare, did you take a lunch yet?" Each contestant was allowed to eat from the craft foods table at any time that suited them since there wasn't a good uniform time to stop them all at once. Bellamy had snagged a quick bite while waiting for the cookies to cool enough to apply the royal icing.

"Uh, not yet." Clare was flipping what had to be her twentieth crêpe. "But I will as soon as I get these all cooked."

"Okay." Bellamy slid over a lighthouse-shaped cookie and placed her brick stencil over it. It had taken about three hours of their baking time for the cookies to be baked, cooled, and frosted. Then, the royal icing had to set before she could start decorating. Now, she had three hours to precisely decorate 3 dozen cookies in six different designs.

"I'm going for my lunch now, if you have a minute can you set up the acetate wrap, please?" Clare dumped the pan from the crepes into the industrial sink as she called instructions over her shoulder.

"On it," Bellamy replied, still bent over and spraying on the last of the lighthouse brick overlays.

When she stood up, she was shocked to see how far along most of the other teams were. The duo at station two were cousins who co-owned a specialty cake shop in Thistle Creek. They were nice but pretty loud. Luckily, once they'd started building their cake, their focus had decreased the amount of whooping laughter. Bellamy didn't know what their bread was going to be, but their cake was obviously the focal point of their design, and its four tall layers were in the process of being sculpted.

Trying not to feel too intimidated by the impressively tall cake, Bellamy turned and grabbed a thick sheet of acetate. In order for Clare to stack the crêpes and cream filling neatly into the fifty-layer cake, they needed the sheet to create an easily un-wrappable container atop the elevated cake plate.

Clare's work table at their station faced the com-petitors at station four. Bellamy tried not to be ob-vious as she watched the married couple, known for their teacakes and petite bites at the teahouse over in Trout Bay, bicker back and forth about a taste test of their cake frosting.

After securing the acetate with tape, Bellamy scanned the rest of the stations. Most of the cookies were out of the ovens and cooling or partially dec-orated. She'd been right. Almost every station had stars, candy canes, trees, gingerbread people, and other holiday-based shapes. Taking a deep breath of the butter and sugar saturated air, she returned to her own cookies.

"Don't be a failure," she whispered to herself. "Don't be a failure for once in your life."

"What was that?" Clare was chewing the last of whatever quick bites she'd grabbed for lunch as she dried her freshly washed hands on a kitchen towel.

"Nothing," Bellamy answered brightly, cleaning out the airbrush to switch colors.

"You're doing great. We're ahead of our timeline." Clare began pouring the ingredients for her cake cream into a mid-sized metal bowl.

"Don't jinx us!" Bellamy admonished her.

Holding her breath, Bellamy used the tweezers to place the white chocolate string of lights along the roofline of the miniature Klein's Tavern. While it had taken her longer than expected to hand paint each little bulb into the multi-colored light string it currently was, she felt the time had been worth it. It looked clean, neat, and adorable.

The large countdown clock showed less than twenty minutes until the bakers would be required to step away from their baked goods. At that time, they had to be placed exactly how they wanted to present the display to the judges. Only after the bakers presented their flavors and story would the cakes and bread be cut and cookies plated up for individual servings for each of the six judges.

On Clare's side of the station, the stollen bread was fully cooled and drizzled with a cinnamon almond icing. Now, Clare was carefully removing the acetate to do the smooth frosting finish on the fifty-layer cake.

"Excuse me, station three? Nothin' But Sugar?" Sharla, the production assistant appeared at the edge of the table.

"Yes, that's us," Clare answered

Bellamy set down the tweezers, stretching her neck and hands.

"I'm so sorry to interrupt, but you have a phone call. They're asking for Bellamy, specifically."

The sisters exchanged glances, and Bellamy answered, 'I'll take it. You keep working."

"I'm so sorry to interrupt the decorating, it's just that they said it was urgent and she sounded panicked," Sharla spoke quietly as she led Bellam quickly off the set and into the interview room, where a phone was waiting.

"She?" Bellamy frowned, worry for her mother clawing its way into her lungs. Turning away from the camera in the room, she picked up the phone. "Hello?"

"Aunty Baa Baa! I know you're super busy, but like we are in crisis mode and it's really terrible." Olivia sounded like she had been crying.

"Livvy? How'd you get this number? What's in crisis mode? Where's your father?" Bellamy wasn't sure which question was more important.

"Mom left it just in case of an emergency and this is one!"

"Deep breath. What's going on?" Bellamy felt the minutes left in the contest ticking away.

"Miss Everly is sick, she has food poisoning and she can't come in and there is a pile of costumes on the table with pins in them and nobody really knows what to do."

Bellamy's heart sank. Already badly short-staffed, the production couldn't afford to lose their costumer on opening night. "Okay. Okay." She took her own deep breath and asked, "Is your dad there? Can he come and get me?"

"Thank you, thank you, thank you! Yes, yes, I'll send him now. I love you, a bushel and a peck!"

"And a hug around the neck. See you soon, kiddo." Bellamy swallowed hard and turned to Sharla. "Is there anything in the rules about if the assistant leaves before judging?"

Sharla held up a finger and asked the question quietly into her headset while leading Bellamy back through the maze of cameras and monitors to the kitchen set. The clock now showed ten minutes left in the competition. Bellamy was sure she could finish the last pieces of tiny holiday decor on her cookies in ten minutes.

"No. No penalty. As long as the baker is present to participate in the introduction and judging, the team will not be breaking any rules."

"Good. Thanks Sharla." Bellamy washed her hands as quickly as she could and explained to Clare why she had to leave.

"But you'll miss the judging." Clare frowned as she placed the thin chocolate trees Bellamy had created earlier around the base of the cake. "And you definitely can't drive in the snow."

"Kev is picking me up. You don't need me for the judging." Bellamy slid the final sheet of acetate with little pine wreaths over and picked up the tweezers.

"I'll join you guys at the theater as soon as I can." Clare was still frowning.

Chapter Nineteen

Complete chaos greeted Bellamy when she entered through the purple door. Actors and actresses in varying stages of pre-show makeup were digging through piles of clothing or shoving hangers around on rolling wardrobe racks. Olivia was at a sewing machine, eyes red-rimmed. Her friend Melanie sat next to her holding up a list and trying to be heard over the confusion.

Joy burst into the room behind Bellamy. "Oh thank goodness! I tried to call you early this morning to see if you could help, but then I remembered the baking contest."

"Oh, is this your number?" Bellamy held up the mysterious missed call.

"Yes."

"It's not local."

"No, it's a Kalamazoo number. I'm just here on sabbatical this semester. I teach theater at the university." She raised her arms over her head, waving them as she yelled, "Attention! Attention!"

It took a few moments, but eventually, the room quieted and the occupants faced their stage manager.

"I need men in the men's room for hair and makeup. Women, stay here and get the final costume alterations. Miss Everly, as you can see, will be out sick today. You can see Bellamy for her to complete the work Miss Everly had planned on doing today." She checked her watch. "We are at one and half hours until places. Forty-five minutes until doors open. If anybody needs anything from the lobby or a car, now is the ideal time to do that."

Once the men had filed out, Bellamy got costumes re-sorted on hangers and into piles, then turned to face the line of women waiting. Many had curlers in their hair, or had the base of their makeup on, but hadn't yet played up their facial features.

"Melly, may I have the list please?"

"Yes!" The teen handed over the list. "Can Livvy and I go get our hair done?"

"Absolutely, I've got this." Bellamy gave Olivia a quick hug as she stepped away from the sewing machine. The teens were both still in their school clothes. "You two just focus on your big night."

"Miss, my dress ripped at the waist." The woman playing the Ghost of Christmas Present turned and presented the tear beside the hidden zipper in her dress, along the side seam.

"Okay, yes. Take it off, I'll fix it now for you. Is that the only concern for your costume?" Bellamy skimmed down the list Miss Everly had left for herself, wishing the old woman's handwriting was just a little bit more legible. "I'm also going to need the over-dress for Belle's costume, and can Mrs. Cratchit come in for me to get her pinned in place? We're not going to have time to alter her dress today, but I have the perfect trick for that."

Joy popped her head back in the room, "Bellamy, Tiny Tim said only you can put his...dirt..on his face. Do you have time for that?"

Bellamy nodded, still looking at the list of small tears, missing buttons, and last-minute alterations. "Sure, give me about twenty minutes then send him in."

Bellamy finally sat down and let out the breath it felt like she'd been holding for hours when the actors took their final bows. Since Joy had to focus on calling cues, Bellamy stayed backstage to help with the makeup and costume changes throughout. Now, as the audience gave the performers a standing ovation, her stomach started to churn. Soon, she would find out the outcome of the baking contest.

Part of her regretted intentionally leaving her phone down in the costuming room. Maybe there was a text there telling her if she was heading back to LA after Christmas with a pocket full of cash, or if she'd failed again and would have to figure out plan B for her return. Bellamy headed down the hall to the costuming room. The least she could do was get the room organized so that Miss Everly, should she feel better by tomorrow, would have an easier pre-show.

After folding and stacking several discarded dresses, Bellamy found her phone. To her dismay, it was essentially a glass and metal brick since the battery had died. She shoved it in her pocket and added the new, neater, and larger print, tags to the hangers on the wardrobe racks. Then, she wheeled each to the hall and parked one outside the women's dressing room, and one next to the blue door for the men. Joy would wheel them back into the costume room when she came to lock up.

Olivia careened out of the dressing room, almost crashing into her. "Come on Aunty Baa Baa! We have to find Mom and see if you won! Oh my gosh, wasn't that the best opening night ever? Did you see the audience give us a standing ovation? I can't wait to go see the Christmas tree lighting. Come on, we gotta hurry!"

Bellamy groaned as her niece grabbed her hand and dragged her up the hall toward the door into the lobby. She was starting to regret her minidress choice now that it was dark and even colder. Standing outside for the tree lighting ceremony had not been a consideration for her that morning.

"Mom!" Olivia let go of Bellamy and threw her arms around her mom and then her dad. She beamed as Adrien held out a giant bouquet.

Hanging back, Bellamy watched for a moment. She would have missed this if she'd been in LA. She'd probably be just as tired and have worked as many hours on some photoshoot for an online holiday ad. But would she be as happy? With her stomach in knots, Bellamy studied Clare's face as she motioned her over. If there was a clue to the winner of the contest displayed there, Bellamy couldn't see it.

"Now or never, Bells," she muttered to herself, and threw on a big smile, joining her family.

Clare and Kevin exchanged looks, and then Clare broke into a grin. "Baby Belly, you're fifty thousand dollars richer!"

Kevin whooped and spun Clare around, then turned and spun Olivia around too. "You get new windows, you get new windows, everyone gets new windows!"

Adrien pulled Bellamy in for a hug as well. "Pretty amazing, Bellamy. Not bad at all."

Bellamy blinked, mechanically returning each hug. "Fifty thousand? Each? That's...we got second place?"

Clare nodded. "We did. It's not first, but it's more than enough. Congratulations, Bellamy. You'll be able to go to LA and to fly back for the three charity events. We did it!"

Chapter Twenty

Bellamy was working alone at the counter of the bakery to complete the last few Christmas Eve pick-ups when Joy and Miss Everly walked in.

"Hi Bellamy, darling," Miss Everly called.

Bellamy titled her head. Neither of the women was on the list Clare gave Bellamy before she and Olivia headed to the airport to pick up their mom and Jonathon. They didn't have much inventory left for general sales. It wasn't that she was unhappy to see them, but she really didn't want to get roped into helping again. She had a lot of planning to do in a short time if she was going to return to LA at the start of the year.

"Hi, Merry Christmas! Are you relieved to finally have a few nights off?" The play was on hiatus for the holiday and would resume with four additional showings between Christmas and New Year's Eve.

"Indeed, indeed. I never got to thank you for stepping in as you did, darling. You truly were my Christmas Angel." Miss Everly was dragging a large tan envelope from her handbag.

Joy cleared her throat. "As you know, I'll be leaving shortly to head back to my university job."

Bellamy nodded, fighting a yawn. Despite the win and the subsequent money, she'd continued to wake up from anxiety-filled dreams nightly.

"What we didn't get a chance to talk about is part of why I chose to spend my sabbatical here instead of somewhere like New York or London's West End." Joy held her hand out for the envelope, then slid it across the counter. "In here is a big part of what I was working on. My passion is making art accessible in smaller towns and cities as well. So, I worked on a grant application and used my time at The Pine as part of the video submission portion."

"That's very impressive." Bellamy looked at the envelope, then back and forth between the two smiling women.

"Thank you. But that's not exactly what's in the envelope. You see—"

"Oh, come on now, can't we just tell her without all the lead-up?" Miss Everly fluttered her hands in the air. "It's a job offer."

Joy pressed her lips together and then continued, "Yes. It's a job offer. Specifically, the grant was awarded to The Pine for a two-year period to hire one full-time salaried staff member, and to pay several temporary positions for each production, up to four per year."

"Oh, wow." Bellamy wasn't sure what to say. "I'm flattered, but I'm not really looking for a temp job right now."

Miss Everly chuckled. "No, dear. We did some digging on your background—"

"Your connected-pro account, specifically," Joy added.

"—and between that and how well you managed the cast and the crisis, the board voted yesterday to offer the position."

"But what about you?" Bellamy looked up from the envelope on the counter to Miss Everly.

"Oh heavens, no. I have no desire to work on multiple productions a year. Here, take a look at the offer."

"Um," Bellamy hedged, reaching to slide the envelope a little closer. "This is really unexpected."

"Well," Joy clapped her hands together. "It's not exactly an enormous salary. But it's certainly livable. I don't want to be pushy, but if we don't have an answer by the end of the month, we will need to post the position publicly. We were hoping to make the announcement of the grant and the recipient of the position before the closing night of A *Christmas Carol*. If we haven't heard, then we'll simply announce the grant."

Bellamy's heart pounded as she toyed with the seal of the envelope. "I'm moving back to LA in about two weeks."

"Look, Darling, you take it home and think on it. If it's a 'no' then it's a 'no' and that's your choice. But, like Scrooge, I think you'd better have a long night's rest before deciding." The older woman winked and turned.

"Here's my card. Take your time, but don't take too long." Joy left her information on the counter next to the envelope and followed Miss Everly out of the bakery.

As the bells over the door jingled behind them, Bellamy swallowed hard and pulled open the seal.

Her head would not stop spinning. With the envelope safely hidden in the bottom of her suitcase, Bellamy helped Kevin set the dinner table. Clare and Olivia had dropped their Mom and Jonathon back at their house, and then gone for some last-minute shopping. Bellamy had locked up the bakery and did her video interview with her potential future roommates before her brother-in-law picked her up.

They'd seemed fine. Nobody had any pets, and Kelly, the owner of the house, was a nightclub owner and often worked late hours. Jeanine, the other renter, was an aspiring actress and current waitress. So, all in all, it would make a good fit. Kelly had been upfront about the fact that they had two other interviews lined up, but that they would let her know within three days if she got the room.

"Hey, Bellamy, are you nervous to watch yourself on TV today?" Kevin added a dash of salt to the pot of chili on the stove.

She laughed. "Surprisingly, not really. I think it will be centered more on the bakers than the assistants. I didn't even do a talking head interview." The full contest special was set to air after the evening news. With their Mom and Jonathon back in town, they could all watch it together. Of course, Clare was still planning on recording it.

"Clare has been talking non-stop about her new renno plans." He poured Fritos into a bowl and set it on the table.

"I know." Bellamy arranged the spoons on top of the napkins. "She's coerced me into doing some sketches for her to show the contractors."

"Rad!' Kevin was setting a stack of bowls on the table when there was a knock at the door. He put his finger to his lips and whispered, "I'm going to videotape it. Clare and Adrien are going to be so mad your mom and Jonathon came early and they missed the surprise. You answer the door."

Bellamy waited for Kevin to get his phone ready before opening the door.

For a minute, nobody said anything, and then Bellamy was swept into a hug and her Mom sobbed, "My baby! My baby!"

Wrapped in her mother's tight embrace, all of the emotions Bellamy had been tamping down for the past week flooded to the surface. Grief and fear, relief and joy all tangled into tears that became wracking sobs as she refused to let go of her mom.

Behind her, she heard Kevin mutter, "Well, that wasn't exactly as planned."

Jonathon gently shuffled the hugging women to the side and stepped into the house. "Hey, there Kevin. Need some help with the chili? Marlee, I'll see you and Bellamy after you've had a minute."

"Yeah, let's give them some space." Kevin motioned Jonathon further into the house.

Bellamy snuffled out a laugh at the perplexed men as she finally eased out of her mother's embrace. "Sorry about that." She wiped her eyes, sniffling again.

"Oh, when did you even get here?" Her mom kicked her boots off and unzipped her winter coat. "I thought you were in LA." She hung her jacket on the hooks behind the door and then paused. "And how the heck did you girls get Olivia to keep her mouth shut when they picked us up at the airport?"

"Bribery," Bellamy answered. "We promised her an extra hour of phone time if she didn't spill the beans."

"Ah." Marlee settled onto the couch and patted the cushion next to her. "Now, I know there's a story behind those tears. Tell me everything."

Fresh tears streamed down her face as Bellamy recounted the entire tale to her mother. She left nothing out, from Amma to Luke, to the job offer here in Treeview and her possible new room rental in LA. She explained her anxiety-filled dreams, and how they hadn't stopped even after the contest.

"And now I just feel so...confused. I don't know what I want or maybe even who I am right now."

Marlee nodded, pulling Bellamy into another hug and rubbing her back. "You know, you've always been my wildcard. Sometimes I think maybe I failed you when I didn't give you a father figure sooner. Or maybe that I finally started dating again when you were in high school and didn't give you as much attention as the other two had."

Bellamy shook her head, sniffling. "No, Mom, you were fine. We love Jonathon."

Marlee sighed, smoothing Bellamy's hair from her forehead. "It's hard, my baby, to know what each child needs. I wish I had answers for you. But, if there's one thing I do know about you, it's that you have to come to your answer on your own. Even as a toddler you were so fierce and so insistent on being independent. Nothing like your sister."

Bellamy groaned. "Clare has known what she wanted since she was, like, five."

"And Adrien had all that drive and talent at football. So, that path was clear for him too. But you've always just been...searching."

Bellamy sighed and pulled away to sit up. "I don't want to keep searching, Mom."

"Baby, you don't have to. I think you know what you want, but you're afraid of it."

"If I don't go back, then I'll always have the knowledge of being a failure."

Marlee frowned. "You are not a failure. You've never been a failure, Bellamy."

Bellamy scoffed. "Mom. I'm twenty-eight and I'm living on a futon in my sister's house, working for room and board at the successful bakery she owns. I spent years, literally ten years of my life, chasing the dream of being an actress, and I have nothing to show for it. Nothing except for missed time with my family, who is always there for me even when I'm selfish and barely respond to their calls."

"Last I checked, you just earned thousands of dollars in a baking contest with your older sister, which she won, in part, because of your help." Marlee ticked off her points on her fingers as she added them. "You also just told me that you got a job offer specifically because of the skills you earned during your time in LA. Skills you might not otherwise have had an opportunity to develop." She pulled a leg under herself, sitting up straighter to look Bellamy in the eye. "And it sounds to me like you have been working overtime while home to make up for the missed time. You have in front you the opportunity to make choices and change, and the most important step has been achieved."

Bellamy swiped at a tear and waited.

"Now you recognize the love you have here, and you can make the choice to accept it. You don't need to be the kind of wild brave girl that runs off to LA to prove that she can conquer the world. You can be the courageous woman who loves herself, even if she didn't get everything her eighteen-year-old self thought she needed to be worthy of that love."

Bellamy looked down at her lap. "You sound like Adrien. You two could teach a seminar," she deflected.

Marlee reached out and tipped her chin up. "Here's the thing, Baby Belly. You can go and keep chasing those dreams, and just be better at calling. Or you can stay, and chase entirely different dreams, and come over for Sunday dinners. Either way, you're not passing or failing. You're just living. And we're going to love you whatever you decide."

Chapter Twenty-One

"Pass the popcorn, please." Olivia was snuggled between Bellamy and Clare on the blow-up mattress in front of the couch. This time, however, they weren't all wearing matching pajamas.

"Catch," Adrien mimed throwing the bowl from his spot in the recliner.

"Don't you dare, Adrien James!" Marlee scolded from her spot on the couch with Jonathon.

"Shh, it's starting!" Kevin, on the other side of Clare, turned up the volume as the contest footage began.

"Mom! That's so cool!" Olivia squealed as the camera panned to the ten groups of bakers. "I see Aunty Baa Baa!"

Bellamy tried to concentrate, but unless she or Clare were being featured, her thoughts kept dragging themselves back to the contract in the envelope at the bottom of the suitcase.

"Bellamy, I didn't know you knew how to do all that," Jonathon reached over and gave her shoulder a squeeze during a close-up of her using one of her stencils to airbrush details onto the Sand and Sun Inn cookies.

"Oh yeah, it took a lot of practice." She turned to smile up at her stepfather, who was a man of few words. But they were almost always encouraging words.

"With a few comical errors such as green eyebrows." Adrien wiggled his own eyebrows as he teased her.

Bellamy chuckled and then snapped her head around to look at her brother. "Wait, a minute, where'd you hear about that?"

Adrien offered an apologetic shrug. "Had a few beers with a friend."

Marlee shushed them as another of Clare's individual interviews came on.

TV Clare stated, "I don't think I would have entered the contest if my sister, she's my assistant today, hadn't pushed me to. I guess you could say I've always been the logical one, and she's the dreamer." TV Clare looked down at her hands and then looked up with a soft smile. "But it's been surprisingly nice being a dreamer for a bit with her."

"Aww, Mom!" Olivia bounced between the sisters. "This is why I want you to give me a sister!"

"Not happening," Kevin answered.

"I thought you outgrew that stage ages ago," Clare added before reaching over her daughter to give Bellamy's hand a squeeze. "I meant it, you know. And not just because we got a nice infusion of cash."

On the TV the timer counted down, and the bakers were fast-forwarded through the final preparations until the screen came to a screeching halt, the judges' table centered in the view.

After a strategically placed commercial break, everybody leaned in to watch the bakers present their goodies. The first baker and their assistant were from Trout Bay, and hadn't interacted much with anybody else. They were the co-owners of a donut shop, and had relied heavily on displaying different donut techniques to meet the guidelines.

The next set were the loud cousins from station two. They were just as loud as they described the sourdough bread, the starter for which had been one of their pre-made ingredients. Their cookies were cute but relatively basic. But the cake was phenomenal to look at. They'd carved it into an overflowing stocking that was vertical on the cake board.

"How did they do that?" Olivia gasped.

"You know, their tables were right beside ours the whole time, and I still don't know how they did it," Bellamy answered, also in awe.

Then Clare was on the screen, the only baker so far to present alone. After she'd described the flavors, the judges inspected the decorations as they had each time so far. Only this time, one woman with short platinum blond hair held up a hand as they returned to their seats.

She waited until the other five judges were settled in and then said to TV Clare, "It's my understanding that you had an assistant when the day started."

"Yes Ma'am," TV Clare responded. "My little sister. She, um, had to leave to help my daughter's theater production."

"I see."

Seven more teams went up, each with the baker and the assistant present. Bellamy felt a twinge of guilt at the way she'd abandoned Clare. But, the judges' comments had been very positive.

In fact, when they tallied the scores, Nothin' But Sugar had tied for second with the cake cousins. Just before cutting to another commercial, it was announced that there could not be a tie, and the judges would need a private discussion.

After the ad break, the show jumped to the private room where the judges were in conference.

"We need a tie-breaker," The woman with platinum hair began the discussion.

"That cake was an absolute feat. It defied gravity," One balding man started.

"Oh, but the Stollen bread. The candied citrus was so unique."

"They did have the most unique theming." A petite woman with her hair in a braid crown added.

"I feel I need to see the footage of when the assistant left."

Bellamy, watching from the living room floor, looked over at Clare in a panic. She couldn't remember what she'd said on the phone, but she hadn't realized she was being recorded.

Sharla appeared on the screen, holding a monitor for the judges. The screen panned in, and the conversation between Olivia and Bellamy played over the speakers.

"Whoa! I'm on TV!" Olivia squirmed in delight. "I mean, kind of."

The woman, who was clearly the leader of the judges nodded as the camera zoomed back in on her face. "I am of the opinion that as a local contest, seeing somebody unhesitatingly sacrifice their own big moment to help another group in their community, that for me, is what we are all about."

"It is the holidays. And we did rate them equally on the flavors. I am inclined to agree."

"Yes. Community matters, especially during the holidays."

"Oh my gosh, so I basically won the money for you guys by panicking and calling Aunty Baa Baa!" Olivia cackled at her joke.

"Something like that," Clare answered dryly.

"I'm so proud of my girls," Marlee clapped from the couch as the cameras panned to the winning teams during the announcement. "Well done!"

As the credits rolled, Kevin turned down the volume and Jonathon began folding the blankets that lived on the back of the couch.

"Hey," Bellamy licked her lips nervously as she called for attention. "I, um. I want to talk to you about something." She slid across the wood floors in her fuffy socks and grabbed the envelope from her suitcase. When she returned to the living room, the air mattress was mostly deflated, and everybody paused in their cleaning.

"What's up, Belly B?" Adrien held a stack of popcorn bowls.

"Well," she paused, searching deep down in herself before nodding decisively. "I guess I just wanted to tell you guys about something. And, um, Adrien...I'm going to need your realtor skills to help me find an apartment."

"In LA?" Adrien raised his eyebrows. "I don't think I'll be much help."

"No....er. Here. In Treeview."

Chapter Twenty-Two

"Aunty Baa Baa! Wakey wakey! It's Christmas morning!" Olivia shook Bellamy's shoulders.

Bellamy cracked one eye and didn't try to fight the smile that pulled at her mouth. She'd slept through the entire night, peacefully.

"Come on, Mom's got cinnamon rolls in the oven. It's already, like, nine in the morning."

Bellamy stretched and slung her feet off the side of the futon. "You know, sometimes people just like to wake up on their own."

"Uncle Adrien is going to be here as soon as he drops off Uncle Luke at the airport, and then it's present time!" Olivia skipped out of the room, leaving the door open.

Bellamy's stomach flipped at the mention of Luke. He was scheduled to fly to Colorado today, for the next two weeks. With a little luck, she'd be settled into her own place by the time he got back and she could reach out. If he still wanted to hear from her.

Glancing at her phone, she saw an email notification. It was from Kelly, the owner of the house she'd interviewed for a room in. "Hi Bellamy," she read out aloud, "Thanks again for taking the time to meet us yesterday. Unfortunately, we decided to go in a different direction." Bellamy blinked and then deleted the email. If she'd needed more signs from the universe that staying was the right choice, this was a big flashing neon one.

"Morning," She called into the kitchen as she shuffled past, toothbrush and toothpaste in hand.

"Morning Baby Belly! Merry Christmas!" Clare replied before dissolving into giggles as Kevin, dressed as Santa, rubbed his fake beard all over her face.

"Ew, gross, get a room," Olivia crowed, even as she snapped photos on her phone.

Shaking her head, Bellamy closed the bathroom door and splashed water on her face. A full night's sleep, a plan, a full bank account, her family surrounding her. It was the most magical Christmas she'd had in years.

Humming happily, Bellamy brushed and flossed and pulled her hair back in two braids. When she came out, her Mom and Jonathon had arrived and were plating fresh cinnamon rolls. The house smelled amazing.

As she put her toothbrush back in her room, her phone, still on the edge of the bed, lit up with a text message. It was from Adrien. "If you're going to be late, I'm making you break the news to Olivia," she muttered at her brother's photo on the screen before swiping it open.

Belly B, can you come help me bring presents inside?

On my way, she typed back, pulling on her high school hoodie.

"Adrien's here," She called as she stepped into a pair of boots and headed outside.

"Whoa, hey, take it easy." Adrien, his arms loaded with gifts, side-stepped her just before they collided. "There's more in the jeep." He tipped his head back to indicate behind him.

"Sorry, sorry." She trotted down the steps, then skidded to a halt.

There, leaning against the jeep and watching her with heavy green eyes, was Luke.

"Oh, hey."

"Hey Bells. Look, I know I said radio silence until it felt less awkward, but I didn't want to leave before saying goodbye." He shrugged on shoulder.

"I..." Bellamy stepped closer, so they were at a more conversational distance. "You're coming back in about two weeks right?"

Luke nodded, his hand stuffed in the pockets of his tan Carhart coat. "Yeah, but Adrien mentioned that you're planning to leave Clare's house by the New Year, so..."

"Adrien," Bellamy hissed. She was going to enjoy interfering in his love life in retaliation this coming year. She swiped her bangs off her forehead and sighed. "I am. I mean, I was waiting to tell you when you came back, because, you know. I don't want to put any pressure on you."

Luke raised an eyebrow, "I appreciate you respecting my boundaries, but I'd regret not getting to see you in person one more time before you leave."

"I—no. That's not what I meant. Adrien, the blabbermouth, is helping me find an apartment here. In Treeview. I...I'm staying."

Luke pulled his hand from his pockets and straightened up. "I watched the contest on TV last night. You got the start-up money you needed. I figured you'd be knee-deep in plans by now."

Bellamy met his eyes and shook her head slowly. "I'm just as surprised as you are. I just...I don't want to leave. I don't want to miss out on time with people I love. I'm still working through it, but I think I'm okay with leaving LA without necessarily being a big name."

Luke stepped closer, closing the distance between them. "Really?"

She nodded, her heart lifting at the vulnerable softness in his gaze. "Like I said, no pressure. I don't want us to start with so much big meaning. I figured, maybe we could go on a date or two after I'm settled into my new job...or, you know," she winced, "it's okay if you're not interested, too."

"Not interested? Bells," He framed her face with his hands, resting his forehead on hers. "I'm more than interested."

"Yeah?"

"Yes. And I'm not wasting another chance to do this." He brushed his lips against hers.

Bellamy wrapped her arms around his neck, her heart singing its joy in double time, and deepened the kiss.

Clapping and cheering erupted from the porch behind them.

Bellamy smiled, keeping him close. "Merry Christmas, Luke."

"Merry Christmas, Bells."

Epilogue

"What time do the fireworks start again?" Bellamy shoved an ice pack into the picnic basket beside the tuna mac salad.

"Just after sunset," Clare answered, checking her phone. "Which is eight tonight." She boxed up an apple pie, and then called, "Olivia! Text Melanie and let her know if she wants a ride, we're heading out in ten."

"Got it!" Olivia called from the storage room, where she was gathering utensils.

"You sure you're good to finish up here?"

"I got it, Clare Clare the Mother Bear," Bellamy unfolded a bakery box and set it beside the cookies. "I'll just add the luster dust coating, and then Luke and I will deliver this last order on our way to the beach."

As if on cue, Luke strolled through the bakery door, keys in hand. "Kev and Adrien got the grill loaded up."

"Hi Uncle Luke," Olivia high-fived him as she passed to grab a loaf of bread from the new shelves in the lobby.

"Ladies need a hand loading the van?"

"You are a saint," Clare responded, indicating the picnic basket and other packed bags for their Fourth of July beach party.

Bellamy snuck a glance at his bare arms as he lifted the bags, then returned her attention to the cookies. She'd have plenty of opportunity to openly admire him on the beach. Maybe she'd even slather sunscreen all over him.

Humming, she washed her hands and selected the blue luster dust from the shelf by the airbrush. She and Clare offered custom cookie orders once a month now, and these little firework cookies were the last of the four orders they'd accepted for the summer holiday. With auditions for the third play of the year at The Pine scheduled next weekend, it was perfect timing.

"Need any help, Bells?" Luke asked as he re-entered from the back door.

"I'm good. Almost done. Can you lock up? This will only take about two more minutes."

After he'd locked the door, Luke leaned up against the counter beside her.

"Sorry, almost done." She tapped out the blue luster dust and grabbed the silver.

Luke's green eyes danced as he replied, "Take your time, Bells. I could watch you create art all day long and never regret a minute of it."

She turned and smiled, leaning in for a quick kiss.

Luke's hands slid into her hair and the airbrush clattered to the counter as she placed a hand on his chest. He murmured against her lips, "Do you think anyone would notice if we were about an hour late?"

Bellamy snickered and kissed him again before pulling away. "I think my customer might notice. But that doesn't mean we can't park somewhere and make out like high schoolers before joining everyone at the lake."

"That's my girl," Luke responded as Bellamy picked the airbrush up again.

Puffing silver glitz with the star stencil, Bellamy thanked her own lucky stars that she'd stayed.

Acknowledgements

This book, while it has a romantic aspect to it, is first and foremost a love letter to family. When I set out to create Bellamy's story, I wasn't expecting to find myself knee-deep in sibling relationships. But, ultimately, I couldn't tell the story of Bellamy without them.

When writing a book, I tend to disappear in some places of my life and reappear more in others. I am so grateful to the people in my life who step up and cheerlead whichever place I am in.

My mother was of great help in this process as I sent her chapters with the plea: "Tell me honestly Is this too boring?"

Many thanks to my husband, who took several turns doing my least favorite (and therefore most neglected) chore of folding laundry.

And a big thank you to my favorite local cookie maker, @youmadethisforme for answering my random questions about creating adorable cookies.

Regardless of if you are celebrating this holiday season with blood family or found family, or maybe more quietly, my hope is that you are celebrating with love and care for yourself.

About the author

Cass is a certified Speech-Language Pathologist, who is the creator and founder of Phonological and Articulation Children's Books: a sweet, fun, engaging line of picture books that promote speech and language development. Each book targets a different sound set and sneaks in practice and awareness of oral postures and movements for the sounds. The books also work on receptive language concepts and pre-literacy skills. All of the PACBSpeech books have a 'Helpful Tips for Parents" page set at the end to help parents make the most out of reading time with their kids - new tips in each book!

Cass is also known for the Autumn Nights Charity Anthology series that she coordinated for four years. Combined, the series has raised over $10,000 for charities since its inception in late 2019. If you like Young Adult fiction, you might enjoy the "Wilders' series, written by Cass in 2019 as well.